The GREATEST TELUGU STORIES EVER TOLD

In the same series

The Greatest Bengali Stories Ever Told (ed.) Arunava Sinha

The Greatest Urdu Stories Ever Told (ed.) Muhammad Umar Memon

The Greatest Odia Stories Ever Told (ed.) Leelawati Mohapatra, Paul St-Pierre, and K. K. Mohapatra

The Greatest Hindi Stories Ever Told (ed.) Poonam Saxena

The Greatest Tamil Stories Ever Told (ed.) Sujatha Vijayaraghavan and Mini Krishnan

The Greatest Gujarati Stories Ever Told (ed.) Rita Kothari

The Greatest Kashmiri Stories Ever Told (ed.) Neerja Mattoo

The GREATEST TELUGU STORIES EVER TOLD

selected & translated by
DASU KRISHNAMOORTY & TAMRAPARNI DASU

ALEPH

ALEPH BOOK COMPANY
An independent publishing firm
promoted by *Rupa Publications India*

First published in India in 2022
by Aleph Book Company
7/16 Ansari Road, Daryaganj
New Delhi 110 002

This edition copyright © Aleph Book Company 2022.
Copyright for the original stories vests with the authors
and authors' estates.

Introduction and translations copyright © Dasu
Krishnamoorty & Tamraparni Dasu.

The Acknowledgements on pp. 179 constitute an
extension of the copyright page.

The translators have asserted their moral rights.
All rights reserved.

Cover illustration: VladisChern/Shutterstock.

This is a work of fiction. Names, characters, places,
and incidents are either the product of the authors'
imagination or are used fictitiously and any resemblance
to any actual persons, living or dead, events, or locales is
entirely coincidental.

No part of this publication may be reproduced,
transmitted, or stored in a retrieval system, in any form
or by any means, without permission in writing from
Aleph Book Company.

ISBN: 978-93-91047-30-6

1 3 5 7 9 10 8 6 4 2

Printed by Thomson Press India Ltd., Faridabad

This book is sold subject to the condition that it shall
not, by way of trade or otherwise, be lent, resold, hired
out, or otherwise circulated without the publisher's prior
consent in any form of binding or cover other than that
in which it is published.

CONTENTS

Introduction	vii
The Madiga Girl CHALAM	1
The Night After KANUPARTHI VARALAKSHMAMMA	11
Adventure KODAVATIGANTI KUTUMBA RAO	17
Bad Times ILLINDALA SARASWATI DEVI	29
The Coral Necklace ACHANTA SARADA DEVI	37
Exiled MADHURANTAKAM RAJARAM	45
Yaatra TURAGA JANAKI RANI	52
House Number KAVANA SARMA	59
Eclipse BOYA JANGAIAH	68
Breeding Machine SHAIK HUSSAIN SATYAGNI	75
Water BANDI NARAYANASWAMI	81
Predators SYED SALEEM	92
The Truant DADA HAYAT	102
An Ideal Man ADDEPALLI PRABHU	111
Adieu, Ba BAA RAHAMATHULLA	123
Morning Star PALAGIRI VISWAPRASAD	133
Eye-opener CHADUVULA BABU	140
Signature JAJULA GOWRI	147
A Mother's Debt MOHAMMED KHADEER BABU	154
Festival of Love VEMPALLI GANGADHAR	164
The Curtain VEMPALLE SHAREEF	172
Acknowledgements	179
Notes on the Authors	181

INTRODUCTION

In a country like India, with its mind-blowing demographic diversity, the short story embraces the voice of its people, no matter what language they speak. It touches on the lives of different individuals, with their varied aspirations and problems and ways of solving them, highlighting the essentiality of contrast and diversity. After India's independence, new voices, hitherto unheard, emerged.

For more than half a century, writers from communities that were left behind have been narrating the story of their social condition and conflict through prose and verse. This process of self-discovery and articulation acquired pace and focus not long ago, facilitated largely by a proliferation of magazines that gave alternative literature its legitimate space. This anthology is concerned with the story of how Telugu-speaking subcultural groups carved a vibrant voice for themselves in the literature of that language, thus contributing to the cultural wealth of the country.

Our writers come from all sections of the Telugu community, irrespective of their denominational category. Despite the demographic and geographic heterogeneity of the Telugu region, a common thread of change runs through their stories. Chalam was a feminist seer of his time while Boya Jangaiah espoused—as Jajula Gowri does today—the Dalit identity, and brought the voice of subaltern groups that contribute to the cultural and economic advancement of the country to the forefront. Syed Saleem, Vempalle Shareef, Khadeer Babu, Baa Rahamathulla, and Dada Hayat are prominent stars in the galaxy of Telugu Muslim writers coming from a community known for its excellence in literature, music, and other fine arts. Powerful women writers of the past—Kanuparthi Varalakshmamma, Illindala Saraswati Devi, Turaga Janaki Rani, and Achanta Sarada Devi—are a big part of the storytelling arc that begins in the nineteenth century and sweeps into the twenty-first. Dark undercurrents of political and social commentary propel the stories of Madhurantakam Rajaram, Bandi Narayanaswami, and Palagiri Viswaprasad, while Kodavatiganti Kutumba Rao, Kavana Sarma, Vempalli Gangadhar, Addepalli Prabhu, and young Chaduvula Babu captivate us with stories about the 'great human drama'.

It is impossible to select a handful of stories from the overwhelming ocean of creative talent that is the Telugu literary world. This is our imperfect attempt at providing a sliver of a cross-section of some of the best writing to have emerged over the last several decades. We need to caution the reader that the translations are no match for the original. Though all the stories in this collection were originally written in Telugu, as a result of the vastness of the region the speakers of this language inhabit, Telugu is home to several overlapping subcultures with different spoken forms of the language. There are dialects that don't lend themselves easily to translation, like Vempalli Gangadhar's 'Festival of Love', a lyrical love story imbued with the fragrance of jasmine fields.

If the reader senses black and white overtones in several of the stories, it is an inevitable consequence of the economic and political realities that shape the lives of the resourceless millions inhabiting our urban ghettos and rural hinterlands. Poverty drives people to innovate ways of overcoming it that are not always ethical. But ethics offer no solution to the compulsions thrust upon the dispossessed. 'The Predators' by Syed Saleem, set in the Vijayawada region of Andhra Pradesh in the 1940s, highlights the perversions of innovation when two miserable souls vie with each other as they rob unclaimed cadavers of their gold and valuables.

Vempalle Shareef's 'The Curtain' is reformist in character and seeks to cleanse Muslim society of its gender bias. Shareef has chosen, an old woman as his protagonist to personify the struggle against the system of purdah, portraying it as a male invention.

Death occurs in everyone's life and the crushing grief it leaves behind is often accompanied by gut-twisting memories of the loss and the knowledge of its irrevocability. Khadeer Babu in 'A Mother's Debt' and Rahamathulla in 'Adieu, Ba' portray the emotional toll of loss—profoundly purgatory in its impact—and the press of catharsis that descends on the survivors of bereavement with a glimpse into the last rites that follow.

While some of the stories in this anthology might seem dystopian, they spring from necessary truths that society at large must face and remedy. To lighten the mood, Dada Hayat's charming, sun-drenched narrative 'The Truant' gets into the mercurial mind of a wilful child whose fantasy of skipping school devolves into boredom once it is realized. In a similarly humorous vein, Kavana Sarma's 'House Number' gently mocks a self-proclaimed math genius and his convoluted attempts at memorizing and recalling a simple house number.

Several stories, written decades apart, emphasize the resilience of the primal kinship between human beings. In 'Bad Times', writing about the travails of transition during the Partition, Illindala Saraswati Devi discusses the downturn in Muslim fortunes after the integration of the Nizam's state with the Indian Union. The story narrates the falling apart of a noble's family and his daughter's marriage of convenience to one of his Hindu servants. Chaduvula Babu's 'Eye-opener' cautions the reader about hasty conclusions made based on appearances. A young rake pleasantly turns out to be a Good Samaritan creating a safe haven for the elderly, much to the shock of an old man who mistook him for a feckless playboy. In Addepalli Prabhu's broodingly atmospheric 'An Ideal Man', set against a hurricane-whipped Godavari River, a city man is stranded at the breached banks of the river. A poor hut-dweller nearby offers him shelter and food for the night and teaches him what it means to be a human being in the process.

The early attention the state had paid to Dalit literary voices helped douse the flames of unrest in the region by offering writers from the community constitutional guarantees and protection through the law of the land. This is how literature can and, in fact, did mediate between the state and a community to undo social disparities. The Dalit world continues to experience the excitement of arrival and of surviving a history of denial. Boya Jangaiah writes with the brevity of Raymond Carver and the beat of a poet. It is hard to capture the music of his language in English. In his 'The Eclipse', BoJa, as Boya Jangaiah is fondly known, writes of the aching memories that besiege a Dalit poet when he makes a brief stop at his village on his way to court to face charges of sedition. The poet's mind goes back to the days of humiliation and deprivation his parents had suffered when he was a child, a time when upper caste men laid down the law and administered it harshly to keep the Dalits in line. The Rayalaseema legend Madhurantakam Rajaram uses an unusual narrative style in 'Exiled', his artistically crafted soliloquy of a Dalit man addressing Mahatma Gandhi, and casts light on how the upper castes demolished democratic structures to usurp power from elected Dalit grassroots administrators, disenfranchising them.

'Signature' by Jajula Gowri is an account of how the simple act of securing the signature of a gazetted officer to certify that her son is a Dalit, entails the loss of three days of work and food for a woman, and parting with what little money she has to pay a bribe. It documents the Dalit struggle to educate children as well as their determination to rewrite history. Achanta Sarada Devi brings to light the cruel mendacity of the wealthy who heedlessly trample the lives and dignity of the lower classes in her heart-rending 'The Coral Necklace', reminiscent of the Buchanans in F. Scott Fitzgerald's *The Great Gatsby*.

Feminist sage Chalam's writings spanned half a century, between 1920–1972, the most significant years of social change in India's history, the years that witnessed the Independence movement and subsequent nation-building. His works reflect the idealism of that age, the defiance of authority and existing social order. Chalam was one of the first Telugu writers to reject the decorous, Victorian writing style of his times. His prose on occasion pulsed with raw, physical passions that shocked polite society. He was one of the most outspoken advocates of women's emancipation in his time. Like other stories of Chalam's, 'The Madiga Girl' explores and exposes the shallowness and ambivalence of the middle-class moral order heavily laced with its caste prejudices.

Water scarcity is a common woe across India. The water table has fallen drastically in many places and there are dire predictions that India will run out of water by 2050. In many cities, people buy drinking water for daily use from water lorries. Bandi Narayanaswami dramatizes the acute shortage of water in the Rayalaseema region and its exacerbation by political rivalries, theorizing that water and civilization are inseparable, like conjoined twins. Political rivalries also drive generations of cyclical revenge killings in Palagiri Viswaprasad's 'Morning Star' that are broken only when a grief-stricken widow defies tradition and breaks away from her family to protect her children.

The anthology also contains stories of love, that most ethereal of all human emotions. 'Festival of Love' by Vempalli Gangadhar is written in a lyrical dialect, which brings to life the pageantry of the local festival of Molakala Punnami. Kodavatiganti Kutumba Rao's 'Adventure' follows a meddlesome young woman who, through a series of coincidences and calculations, steals the heart of her namesake's jilted boyfriend.

Women writers of yesteryears also figure prominently in our anthology. Turaga Janaki Rani in 'Yaatra' and Kanuparthi Varalakshmamma in 'The Night After' both focus on a man's life after retirement and are fraught with complex emotions and conflicts of love and responsibility.

In the end, the merit of a short story is linked to its topicality and its proximity to reality. Its objective is to cause change and, in doing so, undergo change itself. Thus, the themes of destitution and discrimination necessarily claim considerable space. But the stories in this collection come with more than a sprinkling of the good grace and humour necessary to negotiate the iniquities of a harsh world, while struggling to retain our humanity.

Dasu Krishnamoorty and Tamraparni Dasu
New Vernon, USA
March 2022

THE MADIGA GIRL
CHALAM

It was December vacation when, without telling anyone, I travelled to my wife's village to see how she was doing after I'd impregnated her for the sixth time in the eight years of our marriage. People in the village give the impression that they have nothing more to do on earth other than wait for their end. The fragrance of dew-drenched hay, the greenness of the crop, the freshness of grass underneath, and the music of the carefree birds hold you in thrall, like the memories of your ancestors who've left you behind.

I spent a sleepless night, ruing the thirty-five years I'd wasted, cooped up in wobbly office chairs or lounging in the sagging string cot in my wife's village. A village that seems to have an unfair share of glossy skinned beauties bursting with life. Those girls, the village belles, with sinewy muscles undulating under their ebony skin! When I see them, unable to rein in their voluptuous charms behind their flimsy saris, I'm tempted to prostrate and pay obeisance, ignoring the risk of being flattened by an oncoming lorry, or the call of pending files, or the shrivelled visage of my supervisor.

Just as you can't help but caress a cool, smooth marble surface, or the mane of a freshly groomed thoroughbred, or the hackles of swan-like doves, I've an irresistible longing to stroke the nubile bodies of the village damsels. No matter that they're not beautiful, or decked in gold or draped in snow-white Uppada or gossamer Benares saris, or that their hair is undone, or that they have rustic forms, or that they lack the delicate complexion of their sophisticated counterparts. What man wouldn't give his life to get lost in those mesmerizing curves? And to gawk at the gait that animates their hourglass waists and the pure sheen of their bodies?

They don't flee at the sight of a stranger, or peep from behind doors, or shy away mumbling inaudible invectives when you greet them. They laugh all the time, their pearly teeth gleaming pure white, like the perfectly set seeds in a tender pomegranate. They are not laughing at you. I think it is the sheer joy of living that courses through their bodies, the thrill of enjoying the God-given light and air. It is difficult to say whether the caprice in their eyes is the glint of the setting sun or the burden of the grace of their bosom.

My very first evening in my wife's village revived an acute desire that had been killed by kitchen smells, wailing kids, remonstrating supervisors, and visitors baiting me with bribes. It is not the mundane desire that familiarity and a home-cooked meal arouse in you. Nor is it the hurried act and the stealthy exit after a promiscuous rendezvous that make you vow never to see the face of the wayward bitch again. It is the call of the cowherd beckoning the straggling herd home, the tingling when the cool breeze scatters her hair and caresses the back of her neck. Then I want my love to sit by my side, smile and, pressing her young bosom into my flesh, look into my eyes.

Such a desire is natural in any living, breathing human being; I could never conquer it despite my best efforts. I'm timid. In my village, such thoughts would never cross my mind. Toiling, eating, going to bed, making love, and loafing about with fellow clerks are the things that make me happy. But the breeze here, in my wife's village, is so intoxicating that I can't rein in unruly thoughts. Even God, my creator, couldn't have suppressed them. Not even those worthies who invented morality to deny men and women their due could accomplish this.

You've seen the coastal highway, haven't you? The road runs sandwiched between the canal and the plantations. The sun fills the canal waters with twinkling images of swaying orchards. It was on this road that one day my heart skipped a beat at the sound of a giggle that had the melody of a gurgling stream. I stood in the middle of the road, enchanted by words falling to the ground like rose petals. A song filled the air. 'Does she, the source of this music, have a care in this world?' I wondered. That laughter merged magically with the morning light, the limpid water and the birds' love songs. 'Did this same laughter stir the flowers, the air, and the coconut fronds?'

Fifteen minutes later, she appeared before me like a nymph, emerging from inside the orchards, talking to an old Muslim man and singing. She was in her early twenties and wore a red sari. She approached the canal, hitched up her petticoat and stepped into the water to wade through. My searing scrutiny failed to dent her equanimity. I'd never seen such a resplendent complexion. She wore no blouse. Her sari covered her bosom. One glimpse of her velvety body conjured up a new moon in a sky lit up by stars; all those poetic descriptions you read in the epics fail to do justice to the radiance of her body. A speck of dust has no choice but to slide off her marble-smooth skin. The sun played hide and seek on her shoulders. The mere thought of the curves of her shoulders...oh my lord, ignited the body with desire. The dark thighs radiated a blinding light under the hoisted hem of her petticoat.

My wife, with her distended abdomen, reedy arms, and the elongated neck of a stork, greeted me when I returned home from that visit to paradise.

'Where did you go, so early in the morning?'

I ignored the question and fled inside, afraid to meet her eyes. By all accounts, my wife is a beautiful woman. She has all the attributes of beauty mentioned in the ancient scriptures. She has an hourglass middle when she is not pregnant. She is fidelity personified. I think she would spit at the nymph, were she to see her. But my infatuation with the rustic damsel was such that I'd have readily strangled my wife that night. If I had to choose between the damsel and the office of a governor, I'd be the first to sign a document relinquishing the office.

Restless, I ventured out again that afternoon. The rain had spoilt the day but the evening after the rain was magnificent. The roads were puddled. The trees and birds were busy flicking off raindrops. The breeze romped with joy. The desire to see her had become acute, like a schoolgoing child wanting to skip classes. 'What more would I want in life, once I have her friendship? How about caressing her hand, her curves!' My thoughts hit a low. In my mind, I could see the water flow under the fickle shades of the coconut palms, the grass flanking the cool moving waters, and a strong wind fluttering her sari. The furtive glances of her love-filled eyes intoxicated me.

If this dream comes true, does it matter if I slave as a clerk for the rest of my life, or face an abusive supervisor? I would ask everyone, 'Miserable fellows, what do you know about the sensual pleasures of rasa and happiness?'

I arrived at the orchard and settled down for a long wait. No trace of life. Half an hour later, I saw my swaying beauty returning from some unknown rendezvous. It didn't take long to start a conversation with the simple girl. We start trading pleasantries.

'It's slushy here. Let's find a better spot,' she said, and guided me to the veranda of a factory next to the orchard. We stood there chatting. I was happy to stand close to her, close enough to read the thoughts that animated her face. Isn't it enough for me if her eyes meet my gaze, enough to look at her as she stealthily watches the road for fear of detection, pulling back the inconstant sari onto her shoulder?

'What will the passers-by think of us? They are foul-mouthed. Come stand here,' she said and pulled me aside.

'I first mistook you for the mailman. He often passes this way like Brahma,' she giggled.

That laughter erased my jealous thoughts about the mailman and disarmed me. What was I to do? Could I be content with appropriating that laughter, kissing those smiling lips, touching her tremulous neck, and pressing against her swaying bosom? Why is this silly mailman spoiling the fun? Should I slaughter him, burn him, or simply trample him?

'Why are you chatting with me for so long…don't you have important matters to take care of?' she asked me.

'Because I have a crush on you.'

'What a joke! We're poor folk. No nice clothes or ornaments. Only darkness and crudeness,' she said and stretched her arms forward. A raging desire to grab her hands and taunt her to free herself swept over me, but I held back, afraid of scaring her away. In those ten minutes, I longed several times to touch her but fear stood in my way.

An inner voice told me to act fast before someone showed up and time ran out. But courage failed me. A passer-by might notice!

To prolong the conversation, I asked her if the orchard belonged to her family.

'Oh, you want to see the orchard? Come,' she said and led the way.

I trailed her, watching her swaying behind. Ah, the curves. I realized what I'd missed until now and rued my barren life.

'Watch for carpenter ants, come this side,' she said and pulled me aside. Was it intentional? I was not sure.

We stood behind the dense hibiscus growth. She plucked two flowers and tucked them into her serpentine braid. That tug lifted her bosom and chased my fears and reticence away. I clasped her hands. The firm flesh of her arms resisted my touch. Such delight! Such warmth and smoothness! How different from the married ones who give in too readily, and then act coy. Depressing, my God!

What a contrast those five minutes were! How can I explain my delightful plight? The more she tried to free herself the tighter I held her. But my hands kept slipping. My strength ebbed. The natural scent of her body was making me feel faint—the perfumes arrayed in the attar vendor's shop are no match! Neither is the fragrant rosemary that homeless urchins sell on passenger trains. Her presence exuded a feral scent, a commingling of the scent of the scorched earth after rain and of the fragrance of the musk deer. I would gladly spurn divinity and immortality in exchange for these few moments.

She pushed me away and in mock anger said, 'Please, don't touch me.' Then she ran off to the riverbank, laughing. Was she amused by my shock and disappointment?

I followed her, admiring her loping gait, like a heifer. Letting me move closer, she leant in towards me.

'I'm not that type,' she said, and laughed in an odd way.

My head began to reel. I was having difficulty keeping my eyes open.

Her eyes, her entire body were mocking me now.

'The sun barely sets before couples sneak into those rooms.' She laughed again pointing to some shacks not far from us. 'They've no shame, nothing,' she said.

I was intrigued. Who is this woman? Is this a charade or genuine innocence?

'Men like you think I'm that type. We're respectable folks. Now, hands off…no more mischief. Who do you think I am?'

What does she see in my eyes, despair or resignation? As I stare stupidly, she comes close to me. She nudges my shoulder with her bosom and passes her hand across my pocket.

'There's no rice for the night. If you can give me….'

I averted my face; I couldn't look her in the eye. That statement shattered my dreams. My heart bled at the loss of the beauty and romance I'd imagined. I couldn't believe that she was of the same ilk as the jewellery-crazed, mansion-inhabiting city vampires. But I was not ready to shun her. Perhaps she really needed money for the night meal. Before I could answer, an old woman spotted us.

She asked the girl, 'Who is this fellow? What are you doing here?'

Oh my God, would she complain that I was trying to molest

her? Or, is she just playing with me? I regretted having met her. I began imagining terrible things—public humiliation, my in-laws discovering their son-in-law messing around with a Madiga girl.

'Nothing, he wanted to see the garden,' the girl said.

'What business do you have with these men? Go home, girl! Ha, wanted to see the garden!' the old woman scoffed.

The girl hesitated.

'Why aren't you leaving? Do you want me to tell your father to thrash you?'

'Don't be angry. This man is a gentleman, don't you see? You're angry for no reason.'

'Hmm, everyone is a gentleman. There is no rice for the night. Go get some. Will chatting with gentlemen fill your stomach?' the old woman barked and left.

'My mother,' the girl said.

'Do you really have no food? Whose orchard is this, then?'

'We leased it, but it is always losing money. This year is no different.'

I pulled out a five-rupee note.

'Come inside,' she said.

'Not now, I have to go.'

'Not now? Then when?'

'I won't come again.'

'Why?'

'I have nothing to do here.'

'Then why did you come today?'

The question rattled me.

'I never thought you were this type.'

'What type do you think I am?'

'You'll do anything for money.'

She bit her lip and looked at me with tear-filled eyes.

'Why did you pay me then?' Her voice shook.

'Because you need something to eat.'

She stood silently as two tears rolled down her chest. A cuckoo warbled incessantly. A humid breeze floated in. The dying rays of the sun kissed her hands. Stray strands of hair fell over the flowers in her braid. Her beauty beckoned me again. Spontaneously, my lips brushed her tear-filled eyes. I was happy to be with her but the matter of money still irked me. I made a move to leave.

'You may go but listen to me for a moment,' she pleaded.

'I'm listening,' I said, rooted to the spot.

'Will you come inside that room with me?'

'Alright, let's go,' I said.

She steered me into the room and bolted the door. In one corner of the room were a cot covered with a cotton mat, a soiled pillow, and many bidi stubs on the floor.

'What?' I asked her, confused.

She let her sari drop down deftly and placed my hand on her bare bosom. Would I have pulled my hand back were it not for the smelly room, the dirty bed, and the bidi stubs? Would I not feast on that body? Would I not greedily take in that neck, that bellybutton? Just their sight gave me all the bliss I needed in this birth.

'No,' I said, retrieving my hand with some effort.

'Why did you touch me a while ago when we were in the garden?' she said combatively, adding, 'I'm not as cheap as you think.'

Her eyes filled again, her lip trembled, and she drew back. I did not know what to do.

She stretched out her hand and pressed the five-rupee note into my palm and closed it.

'Where will you find food for the night?' I asked her.

The look she gave me would have reduced any mortal to ashes.

'Are you angry with me?' I asked.

'What does it matter? The anger of lowly people like us does not count.'

'Look, you're angry.'

'Not at all. You may go now.'

'Please accept this,' I said stretching out the note.

'Not if it is charity.'

'Is it worse than the way you make money?'

Silence.

'I'm your friend. This is a gift; I can't see you go hungry. Please accept.'

I touched her cheek with affection and gazed at her. She slumped onto the bed, covered her eyes with her palms, and cried. I knew this would happen. I wiped the tears and kissed her eyes and sat by her side.

'Why do you cry?' I asked.

She did not reply, but I knew she wanted to tell me something. I waited.

'You think I asked you for money for myself? But it has become my job, my living, whether I like it or not. We've always lived beyond our means. I guess my mother used to raise extra money in this manner. One day, she gifted me to Venkayya, a man of our caste.

'We owed him a few hundred rupees. He tried to take me when I was asleep. I shouted for help but mother had already left. My father too.

'I ran all over the orchard and hid behind a jujube bush, gasping. It was a full moon night. He found me and threw me down. I fought him till my strength failed. I collapsed. I closed my eyes and awaited the worst. But I don't know what came over him. He bashed my head against the ground, spat, and left, cursing my parents. I was lying there like a corpse when my mother came and began beating me and complaining that I hadn't pleased him. I told her I wasn't going to allow him to enter me. That angered her more and another round of thrashing followed. "Who'll repay the debts; your husband?" she yelled.'

'What happened then?' I asked.

'Oh, what a night that was! He returned the next day. "I'll kill you if you touch me," I told him. My mother threw me out again.

There was no one to help me. My husband, whom I had never seen after I came of age, had migrated to Rangoon.'

'You must have been in quite a difficult spot,' I said.

'I was. There was hardly a man who didn't ogle me whenever I stepped out. I was too innocent and didn't understand the meaning of those looks. Over time, I began to fear my beauty. I realized why Muslim women wore the burqa. The lecherous looks of these men bothered me more than their touch or illicit caress. I wanted to spit in their faces.'

'Then?' I asked her.

'One day, the owner of the factory asked me to report for the night shift. I refused. "You won't get any wages, then," he said. How do we repay our mounting debt? So, I reported for the night shift. There was no one else in the factory. He grabbed my hand. I told him not to touch me. "I'm a Madiga and you're a Brahmin. It doesn't befit you," I told him. I managed to slip out and ran to his house, not far from the factory, and fell at the feet of his mother and wife. "Don't touch us, you Madiga," they shouted. "What about your son who is stalking a Madiga?" I asked them.'

She paused for a minute to catch her breath.

'They hurled a sickle at me. The owner came and tried to molest me regardless of the presence of his wife and mother. I picked up the sickle and threw it at his face and fled. Soon, the police caught me and locked me up in jail. A constable came by and said he could get me out if I agreed to sleep with him. I didn't. He beat me till I became unconscious. Then he had me. Then others followed.'

She sighed.

'That was it. After I'd lost my chastity, there was no point in virtue, I thought. I agreed to become Venkayya's concubine. He gave me good clothes, jewellery, good food. When he died, I was back on the streets again. This is the only way I know to save my family from starvation. Tell me, is there any other way?'

I had no answer.

THE NIGHT AFTER
KANUPARTHI VARALAKSHMAMMA

On the eve of his retirement, deputy collector Rajeswara Rao moved heaven and earth to win a two-year extension—he even dyed his hair and filled the gaps in his teeth with partial dentures. Nothing worked. Suddenly, like a bolt from the blue, the government sent orders asking him to lay down office at the end of that month and receive his monthly pension thereafter. He called his bosses, whom he had plied with favours. Ungrateful fellows. True, it was hard on a person who is hale and hearty to join the army of pensioners, and give up the high office that one had become used to!

What was the pension worth after all? How is one to suffer the drop in income from seven hundred and fifty rupees to two hundred and fifty, the loss of a retinue of office-deployed servants, and the disappearance of aides and yes-men? And, no more official residence! Worst of all, his right hand that once wielded a ruthless pen to rule the district and sub-districts, was now paralyzed. So many blows! Retirement is certainly a matter to be mourned. To live as if he and the outside world had parted ways!

But why was it so hard? He'd enjoyed the fruits of office, as God had ordained, till the end of his term. His successor was waiting in the sidelines like a hawk, ready to swoop in on its prey. His ascent from magistrate to tehsildar, to sheristadar, and finally to deputy collector, had been dizzying and exhilarating. He was showered with congratulatory messages from friends and relatives at each step of the climb. But his plight at the end of the journey was quite pathetic. No wonder people compare a man's retirement to a woman's widowhood.

Once Rajeswara Rao began climbing up the ladder, he never had to exert himself in any way, even to pick up a handkerchief that had dropped to the ground. He never had to reach for the uttareeyam, his ceremonial scarf, hanging from the peg. There was a servant for every chore. That's how things had been until this day, his last day in office.

Rajeswara Rao, with an impressive brow and large eyes, was an imposing figure and by nature a person who loved to make an entry in style. The outfits he wore and the objects he surrounded himself with proclaimed good taste. When he came out in a mirror-bedecked carriage, or on horseback, or riding a motorcycle, grown men feared looking him in the eye. They instantly stepped aside to make way for him. His wife and children too carried themselves with dignity. Women in his household, unlike housewives elsewhere, never had to do domestic chores. Why would they need to, when the man of the house was a deputy collector? Two cooks (one at home and the other to accompany the officer on tour), four servants and other staff deputed by the government, and many others helped the household run smoothly. Some worked in the hope of winning favour and some in gratitude. His big bungalow crawled with servants, waiting on every whim of the family members.

Rajeswara Rao had always lived in a double-storied bungalow, not the single-storied hovels that the hoi polloi inhabited. And the artefacts in his house! Unique and valuable objects—sofas, chairs, writing desks, armoires, large mirrors, and paintings—would greet you everywhere. The house was a showcase of gold, silver and eye-catching textiles in dazzling, shimmering hues.

Until the day of his retirement, not only the deputy collector but his wife and children too lived in a rarefied world of contentment and comfort, a kingdom of sensory delights meticulously created by the minions. Neither he nor anyone in the family had bothered or cared to anticipate this depressing day—the day of retirement. Their shining days of grandeur had come to an end. Today, the pension order arrived to crush them like Vamana crushing King Bali into the bowels of the earth.

Sorrow and joy are the twin sides of life. People bereft of wisdom fail to comprehend this and become giddy with arrogance during the good times and wallow in abject misery when the going gets tough. As Rajeswara Rao broods over his impending anonymity, waiting out his last day in office, the man who is to succeed him as deputy collector has already camped out in the travellers' bungalow, waiting with unbounded joy and anticipation. The fading bureaucrat's heart almost stops at the thought of this vulgar upstart waiting eagerly at the doors of power. The elixir that had intoxicated him for twenty-five years begins to thus ebb from his system.

In the grip of a melancholic introspection, he realized what a self-centred, heartless master he'd been during his lengthy tenure. He knew no compassion and never gave a moment of rest to his masseur or the man who kept the overhead manual fan moving, nor did he ever have the courtesy to ask a humble clerk to sit down. His life was devoted to the self. He'd used his clout to retire inconvenient subordinates prematurely, depriving their families of much needed income. Epithets like stone-hearted, snob, and ruthless trailed him. He took a perverse pride in owning them. Perhaps, he even revelled in them. He lived above the common people whose lives he ruled. His distress at his disempowerment, at being thrown unceremoniously among the riff-raff that he'd disdained all his life, made the day feel like judgment day.

His house echoed with the whimpering pleas of his subordinates, pleading for a reprieve from premature retirement, begging not to take away their means of educating their children, and entreaties to help them look after elderly parents. Was it a cruel trick played with the help of a hidden gramophone? He looked around the room but could find no trace of such devilry. It is easy to shut out loathsome images and unpalatable sounds in the real world but how to drown the cries of a guilty heart? He felt something close to remorse. And contrition too. Oh God, why don't you take me away before this humiliation kills me? How could I be so blind to my power-fuelled arrogance?

Why can't time stop ticking and spare me tomorrow's ignominy? But time, as its wont, ticked by and the day of reckoning arrived. Exhausted from sleeplessness, Rajeswara Rao gulped down his morning coffee and stepped out onto the porch at eight. The porch was empty and desolate. The orderlies had already gravitated toward the new boss. The concierge was missing. The sofas, the chairs, the books, the papers, and other paraphernalia mocked him in farewell. This is the afterlife, he thought dismally.

He was pacing up and down in his office when Avadhani, his successor, appeared at the gate flanked by liveried footmen, to make a courtesy call. Rajeswara Rao grew pale but welcomed him cordially, though what he really wanted to do was throw him out unceremoniously. The new officer told him that the stars were aligned auspiciously for a handover of power and requested that Rao pass on the baton to him. 'I too relied on these stellar calculations when I stepped into this office for the first time but the stars have let me down today,' Rao thought. He tried to stall for time but Avadhani persisted. Finally, Rao saw the futility of warding off the inevitable and, handing over office to Avadhani, returned home, for the first time in twenty-five years, without an office retinue trailing him.

The whole world seemed to have lost respect for him and treated him with indifference. He did not go to the club. A couple of visitors called on him and left after a brief chat. Liberated from the shackles of a schedule, he and his wife finished dinner early that evening. Rao was in no mood for conversation and went to bed early on his first night after retirement. It was the worst night of his life. His conscience, that had been dormant for decades, suddenly became vocal. 'What good has your long career accomplished?' it asked. He was not able to come up with a single good or compassionate deed that he'd done in office. On the contrary, he'd brought indescribable grief to countless underlings, suspending some, dismissing others, withholding increments and promotions, imposing excessive penalties and even denying pensions. His career had been one of self-aggrandizement and self-absorption. The symbols of his past, the tokens of misuse of office, the files, the books, and the papers came alive all around him and danced in diabolical mockery. They demanded an explanation for his misdeeds, driving home his diminished status with every barb aimed at his heart.

He suddenly remembered an incident from the past. He had been a divisional magistrate at that time, and before him stood the accused—a patriot wearing a garland of flowers made by his followers, radiating peace and righteousness. A mob outside the court shouted slogans in his praise. Undeterred by the popularity of the accused, or perhaps provoked by it, magistrate Rajeswara Rao looked sharply at him and impulsively pronounced, 'Three years rigorous imprisonment.'

The accused greeted the sentence with a gentle smile, unafraid of the punishment or the hardship that would accompany it. Enraged, the magistrate said, 'Fine of one thousand rupees.' The patriot merely smiled another serene smile. Infuriated at this apparent display of defiance, the magistrate inflicted a humiliating order that the convict be taken out of the court in handcuffs.

That patriot was scheduled for release today; what a coincidence! He would walk directly into the hearts of the people. Rao too had been released from the trappings of his office but what was *his* place in the hearts of the people? These questions lashed at him the whole night, and deprived him of sleep and peace. At last he slipped into a semblance of sleep, only to awake soon due to the humidity in the room. He shouted, 'You, Subba, why aren't you manning the fan, have you fallen asleep?' and immediately remembered, sadly, that he was an officer no more and that the servant who worked the manual fan was not at his beck and call anymore. The former officer bit his lip and sighed. Startled by his shout, his wife got up and said, 'What servant are you dreaming of?' He grew red and said nothing. Why should I rue the loss of this comfort when millions of people sleep without a fan every day? That thought brought tears to his eyes. He turned over in his bed and covered his eyes.

ADVENTURE

KODAVATIGANTI KUTUMBA RAO

Her father and elder brother have left for work, her younger brother for school. Her mother and sister-in-law are making papads in the kitchen, rhythmically working the rolling pins. When Rajyalakshmi asks if she can help, they politely decline. Her mother says, 'You're eating more dough than rolling; we don't need your help, my dear.' Her sister-in-law joins her mother, 'There're only two rolling pins. Why don't you spare yourself the bother and read a film magazine?'

'After such ingratitude, why should I hang around?' thinks Rajyalakshmi, and stomps out in a huff. Before vanishing, she gulps down a glass of water and snatches two lumps of papad dough. The spicy dough sears her tongue and causes her to pant as she marches out to the living room.

Her eyes fall on a letter resting invitingly on the windowsill. It is addressed to her. This is the first letter she has ever received! The letter is from Guntur. Who could have written it? Could it be from her sister, her adored akka? The address in English is not in her brother-in-law's handwriting. Besides, akka had written only a day or two ago. In the frenzy of moving homes, their mother couldn't write back immediately, and decided to do it later that evening and post it. 'Good thing the mailbox is not very far from our new home,' she thinks.

Rajyalakshmi's mind returns to the letter at hand and she is now in a tearing hurry to open the letter and siphon the contents. She rips the envelope and fishes out the letter and turns red at the first few words.

To dear Rajyam, my life,

Rajyalakshmi's eyes involuntarily travel to the signature at the bottom:

Yours, your worshipper, Ranga Rao.

The air goes out of her lungs, and she feels a pounding in her ears. 'Who is this Ranga Rao? How dare he write to me? Or, address me so intimately?' As the first flush passes she persuades herself, 'No harm in reading, I'll destroy it anyway.'

My dear Rajyam, my life,

No letter from you in a long time. Life has lost all its lustre and hope, and has become inert like the furrowed earth under a merciless sun. If you rain sympathy on me like cool monsoon mist, my life will bloom again. Rajyam, is this a time for silence? Write to me at once. My luck will turn. I'll get my job back. I'm selling away my books one by one to make ends meet but will buy twice the number again.

To be fair, I shouldn't complain because a job is awaiting me if I deign to take it. Many of my friends and relatives are furious with me for turning it down. For a mere hundred rupees, how can I swallow all insults and serve the most wretched and uncultured people? Isn't a man who sells himself into slavery a burden on this earth?

I sat down to write a song. Had I done that, you would have found it in this letter. As I told you my heart is wounded. There is no music inside me. I wanted to write this letter full of joy but now it is full of pain. I'll be more cheerful next time.

Yours, your worshipper, Ranga Rao.

After she reads the letter her unease vanishes. The letter is meant for someone else. Why then was it addressed to her, she wonders. 'Yes, the previous tenants were Telugu too,' she recalls. 'Maybe, they had a daughter with the same name as I. It was just three days ago that we moved into this house. Even if it were a prank, how would this Ranga Rao know my new address? It won't be good if my parents or my sister-in-law or one of my brothers sees this letter.'

So, Rajyalakshmi tears it to pieces and throws them into the dirt pit outside. She reappears in the kitchen and resumes feasting on the papad dough.

'Darling, why have you come back?!' her sister-in-law exclaims in exasperation.

Droupadamma, a Telugu neighbour from the fourth house down the block, comes as a godsend before she can muster a retort.

'Oh, spicy papads, how lovely! It has been years since I tasted these! They only sell those bland pale things in the shops these days,' exclaims Droupadamma.

'In this big city, it has become fashionable to buy everything. Didn't we all make papads at home in the old days?' says Lakshmi's mother, in defence of self-reliance.

'Where's the fun in doing anything unless we help each other and do it together? I wanted to make papads and fry vadiams but who has any interest in such things these days? How many things we used to make when the previous tenant, Ramayamma, lived in this house! Mango pickles, spice powder, and so much more!'

Rajyalakshmi finds an opening.

'Aunty, were there many women in their family?'

'Not many, just Ramayamma. Oh yes, there was a daughter, of course. She was the hoity-toity type, always buried in books and magazines, going out to movies, and all that. Don't ask me, she had a B. A., I think?...Yes, a B. A.'

'What was the girl's name?'

'Rajyam, they called her Rajyam. Perhaps it was Rajyalakshmi or something.'

'My, that is our Lakshmi's name too!' says her sister-in-law as she holds the papad up against the light to check if it is sufficiently thin.

'What's in a name? There is no comparison between our lovely girl Lakshmi here and that girl! But first, are you going to give me some papads or not? Not for free, I'll pay,' says Droupadamma.

For a day or two, Ranga Rao's letter fills and intrigues Rajyalakshmi's mind. Its sentences swirl in her head and keep other thoughts at bay. Everybody at home notices her abstraction and comments on it. Gradually, thoughts of Ranga Rao's letter lose their edge; Rajyalakshmi stops worrying about it.

Just when this epistolary episode seems to have run out of steam, another letter arrives from Ranga Rao. Luckily, it falls into Lakshmi's hands before anyone else notices it. The letter is brief this time.

> Rajyam, didn't you get my letter? Why didn't you reply? You want to torment me knowing how I pine for you? Or did I unknowingly annoy you?
>
> Yours,
> Ranga Rao

The letter angers and irritates her. 'All men are alike. Weak. Running after women they can't have.'

She knows nothing about Ranga Rao, or the object of his fancy, Rajyam, for that matter. But she has no doubt that Ranga Rao's infatuation with Rajyam was misplaced. She detests Ranga Rao. 'I must dash off a letter to him,' she thinks. After everyone goes to bed that night she sits down to write a brief letter. She finds that it is not as easy as she had imagined. Words tumble out in disarray. She is sweating. She reads what little of the letter she has written.

> Ranga Rao Garu,
>
> Your Rajyam doesn't live here anymore. She has moved out. Please don't send letters to this address. Nevertheless, I venture to tell you that you're losing your sanity....

'Why am I writing this letter? Why should I get involved in this mess?' Lakshmi shreds the letter and throws the bits out of the window.

Three months pass by without a letter from Ranga Rao.

'Our elder daughter is in her sixth month of pregnancy. We should plan for bringing her home for her delivery, no?' Lakshmi's mother asks her husband. Hearing this, Lakshmi turns into a ten-year-old. She has a knack for growing younger. Some incidents in her life remain as fresh as if they happened just yesterday. For example, her first boat journey was when she was a five-year-old. Thereafter, whenever she sees a boat, she feels like a five-year-old all over again. She was ten years old at the time of her sister's wedding. At the mere mention of that wedding, all the scenes of that occasion dance before her eyes. She remembers how she stood self-consciously beside her sister as bridesmaid and breathed in the scents of sandalwood, rose water, and joss sticks that filled the air.

'Akka is carrying her first child! She is coming home for delivery! It feels like just yesterday that she was a bride, radiant with the bridal bindi. Already a mother! By my age, Akka was already married. I'm still unmarried,' Lakshmi rues.

'We can bring her home anytime it suits them. Let's ask her husband,' her father says.

'Don't forget to write to him then,' his wife persists.

'I'll chaperone her home from Guntur,' their elder son offers.

'I'll go too,' the younger son throws in his claim.

'Why should you go? I'll go,' Lakshmi argues.

'Okay, okay, all of us will go, like the *Paramanandayya* disciples, seven people to carry a needle,' says their mother.

'Amma has found a pretext to bring in a *Paramanandayya* reference,' says her younger son, slyly winking at his sister.

'Shut up, you brat,' their mother feigns anger.

A few days later Lakshmi comes face to face with her namesake. The other Rajyalakshmi and her father had called on Droupadamma from next door who had promptly brought them over to their house. Lakshmi is clueless as to why the sight of Rajyam annoys her. 'Looks like a monkey,' she thinks. 'Her eyes are big but not bright. Must be twenty years old, no more. Acts very snooty. The few words she utters pre-empt contradiction. What did Ranga Rao see in this woman? Well, who knows what kind of a man *he* is,' thinks Lakshmi.

Lakshmi itches to tell her, 'I know your secret.'

'Rajyam's wedding has been fixed,' Droupadamma announces.

'Really?' Lakshmi's mother says with delight.

'She has passed Intermediate. The groom is well educated too. He has studied M. A. and earns more than 500 rupees per month.'

'Big deal,' says Lakshmi impishly. She couldn't resist. All that posturing! Rajyam pretends not to hear. Her mother is the only one that hears it and looks at Lakshmi in dismay.

'If you marry, marry someone with a lot of money. Not a jobless person,' says Lakshmi addressing no one in particular but looking slyly at Rajyam to see if she picked up the veiled reference to Ranga Rao.

Rajyam stares sharply at Lakshmi, not one to be cowed easily. Lakshmi's respect for Rajyam goes up a notch. 'She's only a couple of years older than me, but acts ten years older. I must also learn to be dignified,' Lakshmi thinks. 'She couldn't have made a fool of Ranga Rao unless she had that kind of confidence!'

Rajyam's father asks for Lakshmi's father's name and writes it on the wedding invitation card. Handing it to him, he says, 'The wedding is in the city this month. You must all come.'

'By that time, our sister would have come from Guntur,' chimes in Lakshmi, casually dropping the name of Rajyam's admirer's hometown.

Rajyam shoots the same sharp look at Lakshmi as she had earlier.

'Our eldest daughter is coming home for her delivery,' says Lakshmi's mother trying to explain her daughter's remark.

'Oh, is that so,' says Droupadamma.

The visitors leave.

That same day Lakshmi impulsively crosses out her father's address on Rajyam's wedding invitation, writes Ranga Rao's name and address, sticks a stamp on it, and pushes it into the mailbox near her house. She comes home feeling triumphant.

Lakshmi's brother-in-law writes to her father that they can pick up their daughter for her confinement after the twelfth. Thirteenth is an auspicious day. So, it is settled that Lakshmi's elder brother and his wife would go to Guntur. Her younger brother insists that he should join them. Lakshmi is in no mood to drop out, though she doesn't believe that she'd be allowed to accompany them.

Meanwhile, a letter arrives unexpectedly, addressed to Rajyam. The women of the house were about to sit down for lunch when Lakshmi hears a sound and spies a card on the windowsill in the next room, pushed in by the mailman. She goes over and picks it up—her name is on it, but the handwriting is different. She hides the letter in a book and joins the others for lunch. After lunch she sneaks out to steal a look at the letter.

'Where are you going?' her mother asks.

'I'm bored. I'll go to the park—I'll be back before dusk,' replies Lakshmi.

She goes past two streets and takes out the letter. She reads:

To Lakshmi Devi, devil incarnate.

Received the wedding invitation that you've so kindly mailed. Ever since he set eyes on it, my brother is unconscious with 105 degree fever. We'll remember the good turn you have done us for generations to come.

Yours, Venkateswarlu.

Lakshmi is deflated. It feels like the pavement beneath her has sucked out all her strength and an alarm clock has gone off in her head.

Sounds of the traffic around seem to come from a deep well.

'What had she done?' She racks her brain trying to understand why she had mailed that invitation to Ranga Rao. Would he die? Would that make her a murderer?

Her conscience revolts against such thoughts. If she hadn't sent it, wouldn't he have come to know of the wedding some day? This fever would visit him even then. Is it her fault that Ranga Rao is ready to die for this miserable Rajyam? Let him die...but, she could have at least absolved herself if she hadn't sent the invitation. Why had she done this foolish thing?

Lakshmi is not mature enough to know the answers to these questions. We have to admit that she had mailed the invitation to Ranga Rao to tell him, 'Look at what the woman you are in love with is doing!' It's true that Lakshmi is envious because she is not the woman Ranga Rao is in love with, and she has tried to disguise that jealousy. It's possible that she had wanted to cause pain to the man who is the reason for her jealousy.

However, Lakshmi is now repenting. Remorse has the upper hand in the battle of her emotions because she cannot convince herself that she had no hand in causing agony to Ranga Rao.

'I'll go to Guntur and look him up, if only for a minute,' decides Lakshmi.

Lakshmi has no idea what good this Guntur trip would do. She doesn't believe for a minute that even if she were to make it to Guntur she'd be able to meet Ranga Rao. But it might be the only way to pacify her conscience. Meanwhile, Ranga Rao may die.

'Amma, I want to go to Guntur to fetch Akka,' she pleads with her mother.

'Why do we need so many people to bring your sister home?' her mother asks.

'No, I must go,' insists Lakshmi.

'Let's see,' her mother is moved by her daughter's pleading tone.

At Lakshmi's obduracy, her sister-in-law decides to skip the

Guntur trip. And so, the brother and sister duo leave for Guntur.

⁂

Twenty-four hours have passed since Lakshmi's arrival in Arundelpet in Guntur. Ranga Rao lives somewhere in the Brodipet area. It would take about five minutes in a horse-drawn jutka to get to Ranga Rao's place. Lakshmi doesn't seem to have the courage to undertake such an adventure. Yet, she sets out the next day in search of Ranga Rao's house. It is providential that Lakshmi's sister has a sister-in-law, ten-year-old Sarada, who lives with her. When Sarada is going out to call on a friend, Lakshmi asks her if she could join her.

'Of course,' says Sarada.

They leave home and start walking. At her friend's place, Sarada introduces Lakshmi. After a while, Lakshmi rises to go, while Sarada and her friend are still immersed in discussing their school and studies.

'I'll leave now, Sarada. I know the way back home,' says Lakshmi. Sarada nods absentmindedly. Lakshmi starts wandering the streets, stopping people to ask the street names. It takes her four minutes to find the street where Ranga Rao lives. Another three minutes to land at Ranga Rao's house. She stands outside. Locomotives roar inside her head. The house is a modest dwelling. There is no sign of any movement inside. She doesn't know what to do.

Startled by the *trrring* of a bicycle bell behind her, she turns around. A boy her age dismounts the bike and asks, 'Who're you looking for?'

Lakshmi is tongue-tied and shakes her head indicating that she is not looking for anyone. She wants to flee but her legs become wobbly.

'Your name?' asks the boy.

'Lakshmi. Rajyalakshmi,' she says weakly.

When he hears the name, a change comes over him, a change difficult to describe. He becomes still. His face turns pale first and then red.

Speaking with effort, he asks, 'When did you...come to Guntur?'

'Yesterday.'

Lakshmi knew at once that the boy had mistaken her for the other Rajyam. But she doesn't know how to dispel his suspicions and explain what had brought her to their doorstep.

'Will you please come in? My brother has gone out to see the doctor. He'll be back in fifteen minutes,' says Venkateswarlu, the boy with the bicycle.

'How's Ranga Rao?' she asks him.

'He's better,' he says and enters the house through the front door. Lakshmi follows him.

'Come in and have a seat. I'll tell grandmother to make coffee for you,' says Venkateswarlu, with no trace of anger in his voice.

'It's okay. I'm comfortable here,' replies Lakshmi.

Venkateswarlu tarries there for a second and says, 'I think it is only four days to your wedding.'

'No, no. There's still time for that,' she says hurriedly.

For the first time, a smile lights up Venkateswarlu's face.

'It'll be nice if you could step inside and sit for a bit. I'll be back soon,' he says and disappears.

Every second passes like an eon. Venkateswarlu's exit gives her some relief. She should leave before Ranga Rao appears. He has recovered. A weight is off her chest. Why ask for more trouble? She gets to her feet abruptly.

In four strides she is at the outer door as if someone is chasing her. Right at that moment a jutka stops at the gate. From the cart emerges a young man looking anaemic and sickly, with a bottle of medicine in his hand. He doesn't seem to notice the stranger stepping out of his house. But Lakshmi observes him carefully. 'Could this be Ranga Rao?' She has never seen a more handsome man in her life.

A month has passed since Lakshmi's sister came to her parents' home for her delivery. She was given a baby shower. Every day was a day of celebration. Word went around that the other Rajyam's wedding was a lavish affair, that the bridegroom was slightly bald, that he was also a shade dark and short; and that the earth shook when he laughed. Droupadamma painted a comical picture.

One day, Lakshmi, her sister, and Junior, their younger brother, plan a movie outing. Lakshmi is scrubbing her face with soap. Junior is brushing his hair carefully standing before a mirror in the living room.

'Anyone home?' somebody calls from the veranda.

Junior comes out. The caller is a stranger. Junior is struck by the visitor's film star looks.

'Who lives in this house now?' asks the stranger. 'Does Rajyam live here?' asks the young man again when the boy doesn't answer.

'Not Rajyam. It's Lakshmi,' says the boy.

At this juncture, Lakshmi comes out, her face covered in lather. For a moment she does not recognize him. 'Is this the same man I saw emerging from the jutka in Guntur?' she thinks. 'This man does not look sick at all and looks even more handsome!'

But Ranga Rao fails to recognize Lakshmi. He just stares at her.

'Is your name Rajyalakshmi?'

Lakshmi is speechless. He doesn't wait for her reply. 'Now I understand. My brother Venkateswarlu made a mistake. Thank you for the trouble you have taken to see me. If possible, I'll come tomorrow or the day after to call on your parents…' he says and leaves.

Two or three days later, Lakshmi's father asks his wife as he enters the house, 'Who is that boy? He says he has been here before and wants to marry Lakshmi. He says she is one in a million. He has finally found a job and is ready to get married. How does he know her?'

Lakshmi listens in dismay and says, 'I don't want this bizarre matrimonial match.'

Her mother, sister, and sister-in-law surround her and extract an account of what had happened in Guntur. They tease her, saying that this match was made in heaven. Ranga Rao visits the house a couple of times. Each time, Lakshmi's sister-in-law teases, 'Lo, your husband has come.'

On one visit he says he wants to talk to Lakshmi privately. Her parents agree. Ranga Rao talks of many things with Lakshmi. He tells her about Rajyam. There was never anything between them other than letters, he tells her. No one is dearer to him than Lakshmi who came all the way to Guntur to see him. It needed a lot of courage to do what she did, he says.

'A man once cheated by a woman is easy prey, vulnerable to all kinds of predators. It is good that he has fallen for me,' thinks Lakshmi with glee. 'It is good that he doesn't know what jealousy had prompted my adventure.'

Everyone is happy when Lakshmi agrees to marry Ranga Rao. And he is the happiest of them all.

BAD TIMES

ILLINDALA SARASWATI DEVI

It is an autumn day in 1948. Nawab Abdul Rahman, he of royal lineage, is not his usual self after scanning the day's newspaper. His head is full of foreboding. He is pacing up and down the long colonnaded gallery of his palace. According to the newspaper, the Indian Army was poised to march into the Nizam's territory.

Fatima Bibi is sitting under the tree in the backyard, holding her head in her hands. Her eyebrows are knitted together in distress. Waves of anguish lap at her chest, seeking release. Yet her eyes are dry. After a while she cradles her head in her hands, supporting them on her unsteady knees. She has a hunch that the tide is about to turn against them. She is sitting in the dark, invisible to other eyes, as the cool breeze tries to comfort her. Her fickle mind scurries in every direction, like a blob of mercury.

She is startled by the touch of a hand on her shoulder.

'Don't be scared, it is just me, Khasim,' the owner of the hand says and sits down heavily beside her.

'How come you are not asleep?' she asks him.

'How about you?' he counters.

He knows that this tree is her customary refuge after dark, where she sits and broods with self-pity. She knows that, rebuked by the masters, he has been wandering aimlessly since evening, and doing his chores unsystematically. Understandably so. The master had slapped him because he was late in attending to a job.

Khasim is old, with wrinkled skin, his knees bowed with age and malnutrition. He has only one eye. Fatima is as old as him. She was born with a crooked leg and walks with a noticeable limp. Her silvery hair is drawn into a knot, with her sari drawn over her head. Two silver bangles tightly clasp her wrists like handcuffs. Several gold rings adorn her earlobes.

Soon after their marriage, the couple entered the household of Nawab Abdul Rahman as servants. Khasim does odd jobs around the palace. Fatima takes care of the Nawab's children, two girls and two boys, all born after Fatima and Khasim had started working for the Nawab. They grew up entirely in Fatima's care. The youngest girl, Naseem, is her favourite.

The old couple has no children of their own. The Nawab's children are now almost adults. Fatima entertains the seventeen-year-old Naseem and tells her stories before bedtime.

'Do such things ever happen?' Naseem would ask, with her pearly smile.

'Why not?' Fatima would roll her eyes in exasperation.

'Boo, who would believe you?' Naseem would tease the old woman.

Naseem too is fond of Fatima, and doesn't let anyone say or do anything to hurt her. On Fatima's birthday, Naseem presents her with clothes that she has carefully selected for her, and looks forward to the old woman's fond kiss on her cheek.

Fatima always worries about Naseem. The girl is a stunner, with creamy rose-tinted complexion, the glow and demeanour of a Mughal empress, and the physical form of a Greek statue. Her face radiates beauty, whether smiling with happiness or pensive with worry. What kind of a husband would the Nawab find for such an angel?

Naseem takes after her mother. Her father too is handsome. Fatima often imagines how Naseem's wedding would take place. In the Muslim tradition, it's the mother, sisters, aunts, and not the bridegroom, who get to see the bride before the wedding. They'd scrutinize the girl from head to toe before accepting her as suitable for their boy. The boy and the girl are kept in separate rooms as the minister recites from the Quran and gets the signatures of the couple in a register that is kept in the mosque. After the ceremony, the boy enters the nuptial chamber and lifts the veil of the bride and sees her image in a mirror. This is known as 'pehali nazar', the first enchanting glance that binds them forever.

Fatima keeps her eyes wide open when she attends social gatherings, combing the gatherings of nawabs for a suitable boy for Naseem. Is there any man born on this earth that deserves to marry the peerless Naseem, she wonders. She has not ceased to wonder yet.

With her honey-coloured eyes and red hair, Naseem's elder sister Waheeda is cast in a different mould. Surly. She can't stand Fatima.

'Do we really need this old hag around? Why don't you fire her?' she asks her parents.

Her mother defends the loyal Fatima: 'Let her be, poor old creature.'

The eldest son Nusrullah comes in from the town occasionally to caution his father. 'Baba, I've checked the accounts. Our tax dues have passed the million-rupee mark. We must find a way to get out of this mess.' On this particular trip, there was a note of urgency in his pleas.

'The conditions in the state are disquieting. The Nizam is caught in the vice of hostile forces at home. The Indian government is certain to annex the state anytime. We'll have to pack up, leave everything behind and flee to Pakistan.'

These words frighten the Nawab's wife. She asks, 'What will happen to our palace and estate?'

'The sooner this stalemate about joining the Indian Union ends, the better for us. There is already pressure to pay the taxes,' the worried Nawab Abdul Rahman replies.

'Baba, you don't know how bad it is. I went over the accounts with the head accountant. There will be many debts to pay off even after the properties are auctioned,' the anxious son continues.

As an afterthought, the Nawab's son adds, 'Baba, it is time to cut down the spending on the running of this house. Some of the servants should be asked to leave. Let's live frugally. My wife and I don't need such a big house in Hyderabad. We'll move to a one-room house with just one servant.'

He sees his mother's distressed face but he can't help her. 'Let's sell all the mortgaged land. You try and find buyers. I will finalize things on my next trip here,' the Nawab's son says.

The Nawab's heart sinks to his feet at this harsh dose of reality from his son. The servants, never seen in the presence of their master but always within hearing distance, hear the son's account. They wonder, 'How many of us will have to leave? Who'll stay?' Each one of them thinks he is indispensable. The light on the faces of Fatima and Khasim has already ebbed. Fatima is worried about Naseem. Who will take care of her?

One day, Nusrullah returns from Hyderabad suddenly. The Nawab has been spending beyond his means, as is his custom, taking advantage of the clout and fame of his ancestors. He knows what his son is about to say. The family has bought expensive clothes in Hyderabad on credit, jewellery on credit, and everything else it needed on credit. When creditors press for payment at the end of the year, the Nawab would dismiss them, promising to pay in instalments. He does not want to lower the prestige of the family by curtailing his lifestyle or his entourage.

Soon after his return, Nusrullah Khan takes the lavish custom-built car out of the garage. It is big enough to hold five people in the back seat easily. The trunk can carry everything the family needs for a comfortable, long-distance journey. After selling the car to a rich builder, Nusrullah turns his attention to the land holdings of the estate. He obtains the signatures of his father and younger brother, Abdul, and sells the mortgaged land. The parents are nonplussed. The army of servants line up mournfully and listen in stunned silence.

The topic comes up for discussion that night.

'There is a lull in the riots and unrest after the recent ceasefire agreement between India and the Nizam. People are taking the train to Pakistan. Abdul and I'll deal with pending matters. It is wise that you seek asylum in Pakistan,' the eldest son says.

The Nawab is speechless.

He replies weakly, 'Let's leave after the girls are married.'

'Baba, I have not told you the whole truth.' Nusrullah is unable to continue.

'Tell me the truth,' the Nawab says, though he is terrified about what he may have to hear.

'The matches that we had arranged for Waheeda and Naseem have disappeared after we sold the land,' the eldest son says, avoiding his father's gaze.

The Nawab faints. When he regains consciousness, he begins beating his chest and starts crying. How is he going to find grooms for his two daughters? Even if he does, where will he get the money to perform the weddings in the style expected of a Nawab?

Nusrullah regrets selling the car. It would have been handy to take his father to a nursing home in Hyderabad. Perhaps he should not have revealed the true state of finances to his father but there was no alternative.

The Nawab breathes his last the following morning.

Everyone in the family blames the eldest son for the tragedy and heaps abuse on him.

'Mother, we can't stay here anymore; it is not safe. The Hindus will revolt and seek revenge. It's better to leave before it is too late.'

'But leave for where?' the mother raises her voice in anguish.

'Let us leave for Pakistan.'

'What about my children? Where will they get married? We should perform their weddings here in this palace. How can we do that anywhere else?'

'Mother,' he embraces his mother and cries. 'I've not taken these decisions rashly. I can't tell you what would have happened if I'd not acted now. You and Abdul should leave for Pakistan now. I'll join you later and we can start a business there.'

'What about the girls? When will you send them? They cannot come alone, no!' the mother says.

'Leave it to me. These are extremely bad times. When their turn comes, the Hindus will avenge all those atrocities the Muslims have committed on them. That time will come, mark my words,' he says.

'What will you do then? How can you be so sure that things will reach that terrible state? Maybe your father died because you'd painted such a frightening future,' she says.

'Mother, sitting inside this home, you have no idea what our people are doing. They're looting and burning Hindu homes in the villages, ravaging their women. It is better that we act early. Your daughters should not meet that fate.'

'What will happen to our family's reputation? I can't bear to see my daughters walking on the streets like common people. Why don't you kill me first by giving me some poison? Then you can do what you like.' The strain of all this emotion proves to be too much for her, and she collapses. The girls start wailing while the brothers rush to revive their mother.

The next day, Abdul and their mother leave for Pakistan, taking with them the family gold and other valuables. After their departure, the palace looks forlorn and abandoned. Nusrullah wanders around, his heart full of grief, wondering if the grandeur of the past will ever return: the exquisitely carved furniture, the spacious rooms, the Persian carpets, the marble statuary, floors paved with Italian tiles, his grandfather's art collection gathered during his travels across the world. The patriarch used to hold visitors hostage recounting his adventures, how much he paid for each piece, and what their upkeep cost the palace each year.

Nusrullah's aimless wandering brings him to the gorgeous garden. He sighs and wonders if he will ever see it again. It rivals any botanical garden, with its plantings of every fruit tree and flowering plant that could be grown in this climate. The stork fountain sprays him with a fine mist, the paved walkways and cement benches that punctuate the immaculate flowerbeds around the fountain gleam invitingly. The two swimming pools, one for each sex, glisten in the distance. What is to be done with this vast property? There are no buyers, no tenants ready to occupy it. Should he keep it locked? His stricken heart misses a beat at this dismal thought.

The next morning, Nusrullah gets ready to leave for Hyderabad with his sisters. He pays all the staff and dismisses them, retaining a lone watchman. Khasim, Fatima, and Munshiji, the head accountant, decide to stay another day and see the young master and the rest of the family off.

Fatima salaams the eldest son and asks, 'Babu, where in Hyderabad will you take the young ladies?'

'I really have no idea. I don't have the money to marry them to nawabs. I've two very good friends in Hyderabad. I'll present my sisters to them. There is no other way,' Nusrullah says with tears in his eyes.

Fatima is shocked. She demands, 'How can you hand over these angels to those brutes?'

'How else can I repay the lakhs of rupees we owe them?' he thinks. Fatima was absolutely right. After the novelty wore off, his friends would lose all interest in the sisters. They'll be relegated to being just one of the many mistresses in their harems.

That night, the entire household is sleepless with anxiety. Two hours past the stroke of midnight, Waheeda gets up abruptly and stuffs all her clothes into a suitcase. She walks into the servants' quarters and taps softly on the accountant's door.

He opens the door, takes one look at her, and almost faints. She enters his room and bolts the door firmly from inside.

'Munshiji, how much cash do you have with you?'

'Just the severance pay of one year's salary that I received from your brother yesterday, madam—1,200 rupees.'

'Munshiji, let's run away to Hyderabad together. Marry me, please, if you don't mind.'

Munshiji is stunned. He has been in the service of the Nawab's family since he was a child. He relied on them for food and shelter. He is now forty and single, and has known no other life. Waheeda is a college graduate and a dazzling beauty. If the master learns of this elopement, he'd have him beheaded.

'Munshiji, what is holding you back? There is a bus that leaves at three o'clock. This is our chance to get away.'

Unhappy with his continued silence, she asks bluntly, 'What, you don't like me?'

'I'm a servant, how can you want to be with me?'

'I have a college degree; I can get a job in Hyderabad where we'll be safe. Come on, pack your clothes,' she orders him.

After that, Munshiji squeezes whatever few clothes he has into a handbag and Waheeda's suitcase, and they sneak out of the house.

Fatima sees them leaving and calls out to Khasim. He comes over to the window; his jaw drops at the sight.

Fatima now wonders: how can we help Naseem? She is not as bold as her sister to take fate into her own hands.

'Let us take her to Bangalore,' says Khasim. 'She'll find a job there, and you and I can look for work. We can protect her.'

The Kacheguda–Bangalore Express is scheduled to stop in their town in a few hours. They help Naseem get ready, dress her as a Hindu woman, with a bindi on her forehead, and feet anointed with turmeric paste to declare her a 'married' woman. With thoughts of an unknown future buzzing around like flies, the three disappear into the uncertain night.

Nusrullah wakes up at seven in the morning and calls out as usual for Fatima and Khasim to bring his tea and breakfast. But who is there to respond to the call?

The lone watchman, about to walk out, hears the master and stumbles back to take leave.

THE CORAL NECKLACE
ACHANTA SARADA DEVI

The day was winding down. Lustreless, the sun hung languidly between the two hills—a scarlet disc. Everything the sun touched turned saffron—the trees, plants, and homes.

Vasanti stood on the terrace, fresh after an oil bath. She undid her hair and, drying it in the glory of the evening, sat on the parapet. Every time a mild breeze ruffled her hair, the fragrance of the sambrani incense used to perfume it filled the air. A coral necklace of yesteryears graced her fair neck. Her cheeks glowed shyly in the mild crimson light the corals shed. The red sari, the corals around the neck, the vermilion dot on the forehead, and the jasmine bud-like finger tips adorned with nail polish vied with each other to become one with the fading sun's tint.

Vasanti's heart beat excitedly. A cool evening and an enchanting twilight were enough to gladden her heart with ecstasy and unleash memories from the past. She had returned home to the village where she had grown up as a child after eight long years. Every nook of the village and the house revived old memories, of the anxieties, aspirations, anguish, joys, and the pain she had lived through as a child. The pogada flowers she had gathered, the swing hooked to the banyan branch, the games she and her friends had played in the moonlight near the sand dunes swirled in her head like short stories. But one episode surfaced persistently despite her best efforts to push it away.

After getting off the train, she had dozed off on the way home in the bullock cart, lulled by the music of the bells around the animal's neck. The images of another night journey she had made in a bullock cart to attend Kesari's wedding appeared like a dream—the fluttering of her polka dot skirt in the cool breeze, the carefree laughter of Pankajam. She remembered how she had bickered with Anasuya for the red roses near the malati vine as they climbed out of the cart at home. Memories galore.

The last eight years had seen her life change in many ways. Each step forward in time had brought her life closer to contentment. She had passed her B. A. with first class honours after four years of study in Calcutta. Elated at her top rank at the university, her father had thrown a lavish party. Then followed her wedding to the son of the district health officer, who had refused to accept dowry. It was a grand and ostentatious affair. Soon, her husband had secured an important job in Lucknow and she had to accompany him. After a year, her baby daughter arrived. In the baby's wake came promotions, wealth, happiness, and marital bliss. That, in any case, was what everyone had assumed.

Still, her mind became restless when her childhood days emerged from the depths of her memory. She had tried to return to the village several times, especially after becoming a mother. But her husband's frequent transfers and household snags prevented her. Finally, she had succeeded.

The sun disappeared and the stars began to fill the sky. The moon shone like silver and spread its light to every corner. Vasanti untangled her hair with a comb and braided it loosely. She made a garland of fresh jasmines and roses picked that morning and pinned it into her tresses.

Her mother plodded up the steps, carrying the baby, and asked, 'Aren't you coming down for dinner?'

'What's the hurry? Let's wait for father to return,' she said.

Gazing at the sky, her mother asked, 'When is your husband coming?'

'Don't know. He said he would come for the festival if he

could take time off.'

For a while they sat gazing at the efflorescence of the mango tree. Then she made a bed on a cot under the open sky for the child to sleep. Vasanti snuggled beside the child, lost in thought. Her face was awash in the moonlight.

How many moonlit nights, how many dawns she had spent on this terrace—some happy, others not so much. As a girl, she would go up to the terrace whenever she felt surly. In the distance there were gentle mountains, rolling meadows before them, and tall coconut palms here and there, and the two hills trying to embrace each other. From behind them rose the blood-tinted sun every morning, and the moon in the evening, beckoning, enchanting her.

The baby stirred in her sleep, her head pressing the coral necklace hard against her mother's bosom. She felt an inexplicable pain and anguish every time the corals moved. The corals had a tale to tell.

On the grassy knoll opposite their house there used to be the lone hut of an old man, his wife, and their motherless granddaughter, Seeta. They subsisted on the earnings from a small shop. On alighting from the cart that morning, Vasanti had looked expectantly for that hut and the shop. No trace of them. In its place stood newly built high-rise buildings, masking the hills behind.

Lachumanna Thatha was a good man and loved Vasanti. He always addressed her respectfully and affectionately as bullemma garu, little princess. On the pasture outside the hut, she and Seeta would play all day. She was eight years old, the same age as Seeta. Early in the morning, she would bathe, get her hair braided, and go out to play. In contrast, Seeta would come out in a tattered petticoat and straggly hair. They would play many a game and she would sometimes forget to go home. Her mother would seek her out and drag her away, clothes dirty and crumpled from playing in the open all day.

After giving her a dressing down, her mother would warn her not to play with 'that beggar girl'. But she always went back to Seeta on the flimsiest pretext. Fed up, her mother stopped nagging.

Lachumanna Thatha regaled them with tales whenever he had time. Like Seeta, she also called him thatha, grandfather. He pampered Vasanti more than he did Seeta. She loved collecting odds and ends from her house and presenting them to Thatha as if silver and gold and the old man would lovingly store them in his box. In return, he would give her peppermints, chocolates, and sweets. It became a game for her.

One day, she told her mother about it. 'What! Are you taking things from the silver urn and giving them to him?' Vasanti was perplexed and with a pale face said, 'No, I found them, Amma.'

Her mother reprimanded her, saying 'Why don't you listen to me when I tell you not to go there?'

One day, a man selling corals stopped by their home. After haggling for an hour, her mother bought corals of three sizes: small, medium, and large. They were red and beautiful. She had all the gold nuggets melted and got Sankarayya, the goldsmith, to string them into three necklaces. Vasanti had worn the largest coral the very day Sankarayya brought them back.

'No, they won't suit you. Look, I had the small corals made for you. Wear them,' her mother had said.

She had refused and, without heeding her mother's plea, went out to romp with Seeta. The necklace was long and heavy and swung wildly as she frolicked. It hurt her neck. But the pain did not matter to her; the joy of wearing the new necklace was worth it.

Tired after playing the whole day, she went home late. Serving her dinner in her silver plate, her mother had shouted in horror, 'Where is the necklace?'

Shocked, Vasanti felt for the necklace. It wasn't there. She had no idea where and when it had fallen off her neck in the excitement of play.

Amma fumed, 'I told you not to wear it. You have lost it in a minute, stupid girl!' Her parents grilled her and continued to probe into the matter the next day. This interrogation exhausted and angered her and made her cry.

'Where were you playing that morning?'

'Whom did you play with?'

'When did you check it the last time?'

She had told them whatever came readily to her mind. 'I played in the atrium with Savitri and I checked the necklace regularly,' she had told them but never told them, for reasons she didn't fully understand, that she had played with Seeta. She was afraid that her parents would take Seeta and Thatha to task.

The search for the ornament continued late into the night. There was no trace of it. Next morning, the entire household went on a frenzied search. The news reached the neighbours. A lot of visitors knocked at her door. There was no end to their advice.

A neighbour from the next street came and replayed the same round of questions. Suddenly, he asked her mother, 'She frequents the old man's shop across the street. Did you ask her if she went there yesterday?'

It surprised her mother that such a simple thing had not occurred to her. She sought out Vasanti.

'Did you play with Seeta yesterday?'

'I did...some time in the morning,' Vasanti had said, terrified.

The neighbour declared in authoritative tones, 'She must have dropped it while playing near the hut. That old man must have swiped it.'

Amma was convinced. 'Yes, it must be his handiwork. He often asks her to smuggle out valuable trinkets.'

Stunned, Vasanti had almost cried out, 'Absolute lie! Thatha never asked me to bring them. I gather the junk and give it to him. He accepts them to make me happy.' She wanted to shout this truth out but was afraid to open her mouth.

The neighbour scurried over to Thatha's place and brought him home. He held court in the porch and said all kinds of nonsense about the old man.

'She played near your hut all morning. Who else but you could have snatched it?'

Thatha stood quietly, disoriented and pale. What was being said didn't quite register.

'Madam, I know nothing. I haven't even seen the child wearing a necklace,' Thatha said pathetically. 'I adore the child more than I do my own Seeta. Do you think I would snatch away anything from her?'

It was a cry in the wilderness. Amma said, 'Return the thing without fuss. Why are you looking for trouble?'

'But I haven't taken it,' he mumbled, numbed by Amma's allegation.

The neighbour said, 'Look, Lachumanna, be a good man and bring us the thing. Or, we'll call the police…and you know what they do.'

The mention of police petrified Thatha.

Policeman Narasayya was passing by and peeped in flourishing his baton and asked, 'What's the matter?'

'Nothing,' said the neighbour and recounted what had happened.

Narasayya tapped the ground with his stick and bullied Thatha, 'Why do you want to get into trouble? Tell us the truth or follow me to the station.'

Crestfallen, Thatha was on the verge of breaking down. Poor Seeta hugged Thatha's feet and cried. Thatha went back to his hut like a zombie and brought a small tin box that he had kept with him for a long time. He opened it and flushed out a soiled and crumpled ten-rupee note. He told the neighbour, 'Sir, I know nothing about the corals. Still, take this small amount and leave me alone. I'm old, poor, and half-blind. What do you gain by torturing me?' His eyes brimmed with tears.

After consultation, the neighbour and Amma thought it was better to accept what Thatha had to offer.

'The corals cost twenty-five rupees. What is ten rupees? We need ten more,' Amma said.

'That's right,' said the neighbour.

Anguished at the insult, the old man scraped the box clean and took out three one-rupee coins and squeezed them into the neighbour's hand. 'This is all I have. No more even if you kill me,' he said.

The box dropped from his hand and made a metallic sound.

The neighbour was about to say something. Her father, who until then had balked at Amma's acid tongue, said, 'Leave him, why do you torment the old man?'

That had silenced everyone.

Holding Seeta's hand, the old man left the scene with heavy steps.

Vasanti stood alone in the atrium crying bitterly. She was certain that Thatha had not filched the necklace. But she didn't have the courage to speak. She had looked on passively as Thatha silently bore the indignity.

She wanted to run to Thatha and tell him, 'Thatha, I know you didn't do it. Please don't misunderstand.' She crossed the doorway but Amma rushed and dragged her in. Thereafter, Amma never allowed her to go anywhere near the old man's shop.

One day, when Polamma, their maid, was sweeping the room, the necklace was flushed out from under the closet. She shouted, 'Amma, here is the necklace!'

Amma rushed in and was stunned to see the necklace. With a mixture of joy and shame, she said, 'We combed the whole house, but it never occurred to us to look under the closet.'

'It's all the fate of the old man, Amma. What can we do?' Polamma said philosophically and left twirling her broom.

Vasanti approached her mother excitedly and asked her, 'Shall I go and tell Thatha we have found the necklace?'

'Chee, what scandal! Won't people say that we hid the necklace in the house and accused the old man?'

She couldn't understand her mother. Hadn't Thatha suffered shame or indignity when they had insulted him, accusing him of a theft he had not committed? Yet it was a shame and a scandal for them to admit that they had made a mistake!

She thought that Amma would summon Thatha and pay back the money she and the neighbour had extracted from him. But that never happened. God alone knows what Amma told Polamma but the news of the find was not leaked. However, the hurt in Vasanti's heart remained. It always rankled Vasanti that they had stolen Thatha's life savings.

It took a long time for Thatha to get over the humiliation. That insult ate into his fragile frame. He shut down his shop, sending Seeta to go out to work to feed the old couple and pass the days. From their hut, Seeta and Thatha would send piteous looks at her whenever she happened to come up to the terrace. Vasanti would leave the terrace at once wiping her eyes. When she was leaving the village, Thatha had come out to see her off and remained there till the cart faded out of view.

Days and months passed but she never forgot Thatha. She remembered him every time the necklace rustled on her bosom. She wanted to redeem his debt but couldn't for the fear of Amma.

Vasanti came out of the reverie when Amma called from downstairs, 'Aren't you coming down for dinner? Your father is home.'

'Where are Thatha and Seeta who lived opposite our house, Amma?'

Amma frowned. 'No idea. The old couple died during the famine four years ago. Some relative came and took Seeta away. I don't know where she is,' she said, without any emotion.

What unconcern!

She could not relish her dinner. After hurriedly swallowing one or two morsels, she washed her hands and went up again.

Mother shouted after her, 'What happened?'

The baby was sleeping peacefully without a care, pressing a teddy bear to her heart. Tears welled up in Vasanti's eyes. She bent over the baby and softly pushed aside the locks on her face as the corals dangling from her neck kissed the baby's lips.

EXILED

MADHURANTAKAM RAJARAM

O Mahatma, I've been looking for you, my Lord. I tried to find you at the bus station, at the bazaar. On the verge of exhaustion, I begged for water in restaurants. Everyone says this is a big town. But, I think it is actually a jungle! I pleaded with every lord, master, and boss. Did anyone bother to listen to my plight?

It has been three days since I've been sitting at this place, sometimes standing in the same spot. It's here, at this crossroads junction, that I've finally found you.

In your presence, I feel I'm born again, that I have a new life. I've come to you, to sit at your feet, to pour my heart out. I know you'll lend me an attentive ear, shed a tear for me, and sympathize, 'Ore Gangadu, what a sad story!' It is my faith in you that has brought me here. Now, listen.

My Lord, I don't know how old you are. But I guess I turned forty-one or forty-two at the time of last year's Gangamma festival. In all these years I've never had the privilege of your company. From all the pictures I saw of you in books and all the public statues of you, I got to know your profile. That is how I recognized you at once. This place is new to me; people here are strange. They are at odds in their word and deed. I feel like a bleating sheep brought to the country fair. Though everyone makes fun of the jungle, it is better than this town. It offers some succour, a stream to drink from, a fruit or a root to feed on, and the shade of a tree to rest under.

It's not like the jungle here. In this town, I mean. Damn it, they won't give you any work, a chance to make a rupee or two.

Like plying a rickshaw, for example. You can't even offer to be a coolie without the other coolies beating you up. I tried to find work, the work of dredging wells, but of what use are wells here? Every house has running water, gushing out of the taps. What can I do? Imagine my plight when the night sets in. They don't let me rest my body on the stoop. Hostels are out of bounds. Temples are securely locked. You can't even loaf about the streets without the night patrol collaring you and accusing you of being a burglar. If you run into the lanes and alleys to get away from the night patrol, the mongrels pounce on you. I survived like this for three days. Today is my fourth day here, when I stumbled into your presence just before nightfall.

You may ask, you crazy fellow, why did you come here if you're such a nincompoop? My Lord, don't call me that. I'm not a shirker. I've always kept my word. I'm an honest person. You may check with Pasala Poli Reddi or Pina Peda Rayappa Naidu. If you are not satisfied, ask the temple priest. If you don't like to ask the big guns, you may ask the boys herding the cattle. What can I do? It is not because of any mischief done by my hand that I had to flee my village, with barely enough clothes to cover my body, leaving my home, the humble hut that I'd built, my wife and children, and everyone dear to me.

What, then, is the reason, you may ask? Here is my story, the story of Gangadu, my Lord. You'll find my village, known as Porkala Bayalu, beside the road between Rayavaram and Rachala Doddi, east of Danavaipeta as you cross into Sigamalagutta. The moors around abound in broom grass, giving the village its name. The paddy fields at the foot of the hills are blessed with water for three months even if it rains for only three days in the year. Water gurgles along to the cane fields that are visible from the five ponds where, according to legend, the Pandava brothers quenched their thirst. The red soil at the top of the hills produces the best peanuts in the world. And the mango groves!

To tell you the truth, our Porkala Bayalu should be held up as a model to the world. Our four villages are scattered like far-flung stones. Kapooru is where the Kapus live. The Kammanaidus inhabit Kammapalem. Malapalle is home of Malas. The Madigas have their own colony.

If there is a village, there are sure to be gods, no? See, how many of them! There is a temple for Mahankalamma in the north. On the way to the forest, in the clearing where cattle and sheep lounge under the maddi trees, there is the shrine of Katama Rayudu. Sri Rama has a temple between Kapooru and Kammapalem. Forget these gods, they are mere images of stone. We have other gods, three of them, that walk, talk, mediate, cite scriptures, and claim to protect the place. No man alive can defy Manegaru Rayappa's directive or cross the line drawn by Karanam Mallayya. There is no man that walks the earth that doesn't shake in his lungi when President Poli Reddi glares at him. I don't know, respected Lord, what evil curse has befallen our village. The reign of dharma in Porkala Bayalu that has allowed the gentry and the peasants to live together in peace is now threatened by a calamity called panchayat elections.

You know everything, learned Mahatma. There can only be one hero in an epic. Ramayana has only one Rama, not two. There is only one Bheema in Mahabharata. In our village, Pasala Poli Reddi has been our president since we have had the village council's rule in place. You may ask: what will you do after his demise? His son Chinna Nagi Reddi is ready to shoulder the burden; we have no need to worry.

How are we to know that the government would pass this stupid law suddenly? One evening I got a call from President Poli Reddi asking me to show up at his place. I went there and stood before him with my arms crossed humbly across my chest.

'Do you know why I've sent for you?' he said.

'How am I, a lowly cattle herder, to know what is on your mind, my master?'

'Times are changing. We have a new rule now. None of us can be panchayat president—it has to be one from you. And, you can't say no. I spoke to Karanam and Manegaru. Both of them agree that you're a good candidate. You're to be the new sarpanch, the mayor.'

I was awestruck. 'Sarpanch! What is that, my lord? I've never heard of such a thing.'

'Nothing new, it is just old wine in new bottles. The word president has lost its shine. It is sarpanch from now on. It is the same idea. You're the president of our panchayat from now. That's the deal, understand?'

I was paralyzed, incapable of speech or thought. I stood slack-jawed, waiting for the punchline of the joke. How can I, Asadi Gangadu, who does the bidding of the lords of the village at a mere signal from them, suddenly become a sarpanch just because the government wanted it? Even if Poli Reddi wants me to be one, how can I agree? Tell me, Mahatma, can we drape the goddess in the temple with some rag instead of the finest silk?

I tried a lot to get this idea out of Poli Reddi's head. He wouldn't listen.

'Okay Ganga, there is no point in debating this, it has to happen. You're the sarpanch. That's final. First try to learn how to scribble your signature,' said Poli Reddi and went back into his house.

I felt as if a big stone had fallen on my head. There were so many prominent people in the village, why should this pestilence wrap itself around my neck? What will I do if some officer asks me to sign 'this' paper or 'that' paper? I'd tried to learn the alphabet twenty years ago at night school. I'd borrowed a pen from the boy next door. The brat laughed hysterically at my scribbles until I finally figured out that I'd written Gandu* instead of Gangadu.

But look at my bad luck, Mahatma! The day I'd dreaded arrived one fine morning, bringing with it suited and booted government

---

*a**hole

officials. A messenger came running to my hut, 'There is a meeting in the evening. You are requested to attend.' With my heart in my mouth, I went to the panchayat office and stood there. I stood talking to Manegaru for a while when an officer approached me and said, 'Please come in,' and showed me to a chair. How can I sit, I asked myself, in the presence of village elite like President Poli Reddi, Karanam Mallayya, Manegaru Rayappa Naidu?

No, no. I'll stand here, I told them. But the man insisted until I finally sat in the chair. I was trembling and sweating all over. My mouth was dry. I had no idea what happened in the next half an hour. Pasala Chinna Nagi Reddi, Pachipulusu Chengayya, Kadiri Narasappa, Mutirevula Nancharu, and four or five other 'numbers' also sat down. We affixed our signatures wherever the officer told us to. He read aloud the oath of office and we repeated after him like parrots.

'Okay, it's done. You are now the panchayat sarpanch,' they proclaimed loudly. God alone knows what I'd become and why.

What I remember clearly is that when I went home, the mud walls were still made of mud, they hadn't changed. The roof covered with reeds was still there, as was the bamboo door. The dented tin vessels in the kitchen had not disappeared. The gruel cooked in them looked and smelt the same. My wife appeared in the usual tatters. There were more patches on my children's shirts than ever. What had changed, then?

∽

'You've become a sarpanch, man. Do they pay you a salary?' my wife Rangi asked after we had dinner that night and retired to bed.

'If there was a salary somebody would have certainly mentioned it. I doubt there is any…' I said.

'Well, salary or no salary, you're now the sarpanch. You can't be seen doing the work of a casual labourer anymore. Stay at home. I'll go out and work,' Rangi said.

I was overwhelmed. Chee, chee, how can I live off the earnings of a woman? Am I to sit around swatting flies at home? What kind of life is this?

Next morning, everyone in the village went out to work. I sat alone, resting on the string cot. Everyone said, 'You're the sarpanch. You shouldn't be working like a common day labourer.' I should curse God for giving me this unsolicited blessing and tying me down to my cot, hand and foot. Why should I blame these men?

A whole month passed. This can't continue, I decided, and rushed out to the village centre where I ran into the village triumvirate.

'Are you happy, Ganga?' asked Karanam Mallayya.

'Happy, sir? Nobody gives me any work. We are not able to run the household with the earnings of my wife. I don't have ten rupees to buy notebooks for my schoolgoing boy. I think I will go mad! I can't sit around like this. If you will permit me, I'll go to Rayavaram or Rachala Doddi and try and make a few rupees,' I said.

'Oh my! Don't do such a thing,' said China Pedda Rayappa. 'What if the people in the neighbouring villages start taunting us that Porkala Bayalu's mayor is hustling for menial jobs in their villages? What will we do then? Go to Chittoor. It is a big town; no one will care who you are. What do you say, Karanam?' he said.

'That sounds like a good idea, Ganga,' said Karanam Mallayya. 'You might have to come back and attend committee meetings once in a while. Don't worry. Try to find a respectable gentleman in the town whose address you can use. Cloth merchant Subbaramayya is a good man. We will send a letter to you addressed, "Asadi Gangadu, care of cloth merchant Subbaramayya". You can come attend the meeting and go back afterwards. Do you understand, Ganga?'

I nodded blindly and set out for Chittoor. There is no shortage of gentlemen in this town. But I couldn't find anyone who would pay attention to me. But I found you here at least. You are the greatest saviour of all. I'm told that you devoted your entire life for our uplift. It is you who christened us Harijans, people of God. It is my good fortune that I could find you after just three days of wearing out the soles of my feet. Will you allow me to use your address, 'Asadi Gangadu, care of Mahatma Gandhi, crossroads junction, Chittoor'?

Mahatma, why don't you say something?

YAATRA
TURAGA JANAKI RANI

Venkatrao came home, light as a fluff of cotton on a gentle breeze, wearing a jasmine-white smile. His back, which had become hunched during the five years of retirement, was unusually straight. Eswari, his wife, brought him a cup of water and knew what the big news was, even before he'd said a word. He unbuttoned his shirt to cool off from the afternoon heat and with smiling eyes said, 'Happy days are here again.'

Eswari laughed and said derisively, 'Oh, they have come ten years too soon.'

'It's no joke, madam. We'll get the benefit of the new salary scales now. Arrears will be paid from 1971. My colleagues demanded a round of coffee to celebrate the good news,' said Venkatrao.

He switched on the table fan and flopped into an easy chair, pulling it close to the fan.

'How much do you think you'll get?' asked his wife.

He wanted to tease her a little, so he triumphantly said to her, 'Guess.'

Though she hated this guessing game, she said, 'One lakh rupees?'

'How artless of her,' he thought and said, 'Only a lakh for twenty years?'

This hint that there was more in store was like a tonic and she disappeared into the kitchen to make coffee.

Joy filled Venkatrao's heart as he looked out into the street from the easy chair. He was not sure about the amount, but it couldn't be less than three or four lakh. He calculated rapidly in his mind, adding, multiplying, and subtracting. A promotion and, on top of it, a salary in the higher scale! He offered silent thanks to his colleagues for the assurance that all his accounts would be smoothed out in ten days.

Other than entering them into ledgers, he had never had to handle so many zeroes and had never seen such a large sum of money. He recalled with irony how everyone had dismissed his grandmother's prediction that the stars were in his favour. They laughed it off as a joke. A joke it remained for a long time. The property he had thought his marriage would bring him evaporated in litigation. His father had gambled away the estate he had inherited and died a slave to bad habits. Goddess Lakshmi's blessings eluded Venkatrao. With his pittance of a salary, he ran the household, fed his wife and three children, as well as his grandmother. The cupboard was always bare. He had to scrape the bottom of the barrel for every small need. When he retired, he had a past but no future.

In such a situation, the elevation of his post, and the kindness of a Good Samaritan in the accounts department who juggled the rules in his favour, was a dream come true. When the tribunal announced his award, the senior officers were happy that he got his dues at last. Was this not a reason to celebrate?

Eswari brought the coffee and fried vegetable bajjis.

'Didn't I tell you? God is with us. Bad days are over for us and our daughter,' she said.

Venkatrao was slightly taken aback. Eswari had already started filling her mind with expectations. He checked her fervour and asked, 'What bad days do we and our daughter have?'

'You think we are happy?' asked Eswari, irritated.

'You mean you and me? You have everything. You are a maharani,' joked Venkatrao.

'When was the last time he spoke to me so pleasantly without frowning?' she wondered. If she didn't curb his exuberance now, he might go overboard.

'Maharani indeed, changing jewellery every day of the week

and staff quarters teeming with servants! Enough of your joking. Did I ever buy anything for even a thousand rupees without first thinking a hundred times?' she complained.

True, theirs had been a hand-to-mouth existence. But he didn't like his wife pointing out his incompetence.

'Fine. Take a thousand and go splurge on shopping. Will *that* see the end of our misery?'

'Our misery? Look at our children's gloomy lives. Our luckless daughter, she has never expected a cent from us. Poor girl,' Eswari said in a voice choked with maternal affection and pain.

'Her two children need money so they can go to a decent school. We owe her husband five thousand rupees, the remainder of the dowry. And the five sovereigns of gold we promised at their wedding. He now wants a colour TV and his mother needs an extra three sovereigns.... Her life will get back on track if we keep our word. It is a matter of fifty thousand rupees.'

'Don't look at me like that,' she continued. 'I'm talking about our daughter, Visala. Not yet twenty, poor girl already has two kids.'

His daughter's plight moved Venkatrao. That apart, was it right of his wife to hurriedly draft a budget for expenditure?

'We will see,' he said, hiding behind the day's newspaper.

'Tell me first, when can we hope to get the money?' Eswari asked impatiently.

He glared at her and said, 'It comes when it comes. Is there nothing but money to talk about? You...sticking to that topic like glue!'

She returned his angry stare, collected the plates and cups, and stalked off.

The family began to mentally multiply the amount that Venkatrao would get. The eldest son in Vijayawada discovered he had problems. He had a daughter and a son who qualified for engineering and medicine programs. They needed at least sixty to seventy thousand rupees to enter the university.

'Our eldest son has written that he will pay the sum back when the children start working. He is unhappy that he and his brother only had a middling education. At least your grandchildren should get a good education, he writes,' said Eswari.

Their second son, Anil, and his wife, Rama, lived in a two-bedroom flat not far from where Rama worked. The couple visited the older couple every Sunday. Anil would often plead with his parents to live with him in a bigger house. His wife would curb his enthusiasm saying, 'They won't be able to find a house of this size to rent at a reasonable price these days. How can they come and live with us in our pigeonhole? Let them stay in the big house where the grandchildren can spend their vacation. If they vacate the house now, they can't rent it again for less than five hundred. You talk such nonsense!'

These squabbles were not new to Eswari. 'The girl is used to living with just her husband and kids. Why bother her with the responsibility of taking care of her in-laws as well? Our son doesn't mean what he says. We will not move out,' thought Eswari firmly.

Three Sundays after the news of the windfall, Anil and his wife visited his parents. Venkatrao sensed an overdose of affection in their words but soon chided himself for such unkind thoughts. Anil began cautiously, 'A builder I know has promised a flat in the complex he is building near our house.'

Rama sat near her mother-in-law helping her roll out puris.

'Yes, Ma. They are really fine, two-bedroom flats. They are usually available only on the fourth floor. Your son insisted that it should be on the first floor because it is hard for mamaiyyagaru, his father, to make it to the fourth floor. Big doors and closets, and cool marble floors. So beautiful,' said Rama ecstatically.

'It's a good idea, planning for a house when you are still young. Why should you rent when both of you are earning?' said Venkatrao.

'Isn't it yours too?' said Anil, looking hurt.

'Yes, your house is mine too,' Venkatrao agreed, soothingly.

After Anil left Venkatrao realized that the flat needed an advance payment of sixty thousand rupees and another lakh and eighty thousand in six months. Anil told his mother that his wife would borrow from her office and he would borrow against his insurance policy. It would be nice if his father would help him with the advance payment of sixty thousand rupees now and another twenty-five thousand later.

Venkatrao's heart sank at the hopes his windfall had kindled in his children's hearts. Wasn't he the master of his life anymore? Didn't he have the right to decide how to spend money that he had toiled for? Who were these people to decide how he spent his money?

The money came sooner than expected. He greased the palms of everyone up and down the hierarchy and accepted unscheduled cuts in the payment. In the end, a sum of three lakh, seventy-eight thousand, four hundred, and sixty-one rupees swelled his bank account. He worried that if the news leaked out people would mob him for loans.

He had never kept anything from Eswari. He sat in the chair and took out some papers from a bag and called his wife.

'Eswari, I need to tell you something. Are you ready?' he asked. She glanced at him, then signalled to him to go ahead.

'We reared our children with care, gave them a good education, and a good life. What else do we owe them, tell me?'

It took a while for her to understand what he was driving at.

'You mean…we need not give them the money they are asking for?' She was indignant.

'Don't put me on the spot. Did my father give me anything? What did your father give you? Didn't we give the children whatever we could all these days?' His anguish was audible as he searched for answers in her face.

She stopped stringing the flowers in her lap and said, 'Should we deprive our children because our parents deprived us? When you get this money, give the children what they want.'

He understood her heart now. He pushed the papers back into the bag, sad that Eswari, his wife of forty years, had reservations about his decision.

He said firmly, 'I have already made my plans. I've put two lakh in a fixed deposit, ordered a fridge, a colour TV, a VCR, a sofa set, a double cot and mattress, ceiling fans, and a dining table and chairs. You may come along with me to see them if you like. Hire a cook. Buy nice clothes for the children and their families. I have booked tickets for a railway tour of the South. You can buy jewellery for twenty-five thousand rupees.'

As he reeled off these words, she was stunned. She was furious that he had not consulted her before deciding to deny their children in this way.

'What do you say?' he said. 'What is there to say,' she thought and snipped a small part of the string of flowers. She wove it into her hair, putting the longer section around the Shiva–Parvati statuette.

'Why don't you say something?' he said.

'What kind of a father ignores the needs of his children? You can't bear to see the children happy. You think they should buy what they want for themselves. Such an inconsiderate....' Choking with grief, she broke down and went away to sit on the veranda outside.

She sat watching people and vehicles in the street until the daylight faded. She came back, cooked dinner, called him when it was ready, and served him the meal. Very soon, the sofa set, dining table, and other things he had ordered crowded the house. The house lit up with all the new things, including a sparkling chandelier he had bought. The four rooms of the house looked like a luxury hotel resort.

Anil and Rama visited and were dazzled. Accustomed to seeing the old couple in modest surroundings, Rama succumbed to a strange nausea. A fortnight later, Venkatrao and Eswari's daughter, their eldest son, and their grandchildren came and stayed for a couple of days. It was the festive season and the house shone like Goddess Lakshmi's abode, replete with children, toys, and new clothes. But there was darkness in their hearts. Though Eswari wore her new gold necklace and bangles, her face lacked lustre.

Once the children left, Venkatrao showed her the railway circular tour tickets. She remained quiet with a blank expression.

'Pack our clothes for the trip. I'm tired,' he said. What was left of his grey head of hair, strayed on to his face.

'I'll take care of the clothes. Let's eat first,' Eswari said, sighing deeply.

Venkatrao's long-awaited, much-longed-for moment had finally arrived—a dining table instead of the wooden planks, a double cot with a soft mattress instead of the string cot covered with a patchy quilt. The moment of truth when he could sleep in comfort, with his arm around Eswari's waist. He wanted deliverance from a life of want and looked forward to a time when he could throw money around freely. What was wrong with such a yearning? According to Eswari, everything.

A friend dropped by to check in on Venkatrao's travel plans. 'May I have some water please,' the friend asked. Venkatrao shouted out the request so Eswari could hear him in the kitchen. The friend was all praise for Eswari's sweets as he inhaled their fragrance. While they were talking Venkatrao's aged frame began to sweat. An ache deep inside started making its way across his chest.

'What happened?' Eswari cried anxiously as she rushed over. The friend hurriedly stepped up to him and laid Venkatrao on the new sofa and gave him a sip of water. He had a bad feeling. He told Eswari to switch on the fan and rushed out to get a doctor.

Eswari watched her husband lie on the sofa, peacefully staring at the ceiling with an enigmatic smile on his face. It was not until much later, until after the doctor arrived, that she realized that Venkatrao's smile would never fade and his eyes would never close.

HOUSE NUMBER

KAVANA SARMA

Dr Appalraju surveyed the neatly appointed rooms and nodded. It had taken him a week of house-hunting to find the place. He signed the lease of the two-room tenement for five hundred rupees in Dwarakanagar district of the Steel City. Now, all he had to do was to write home asking Her Excellency to come join him. With that, the day's to-do list would have been accomplished.

He bathed with half a bucket of water, saving the other half for any need that might arise before the next day's quota of water arrived. He wrapped a white lungi around his waist, and sat down close to the table fan to write to his wife:

Oh, my queen, my sweetness,

Found a place at last! Pack your things and ask your dad to put you on the next train; I'll receive you here. I've spruced up the rooms, though not as well as they do in America. But India is not America. When you were there you used to complain: 'There is no NTR or ANR. Every weekend, all we do is crowd into some friend's basement and see a movie. How about watching it in the comfort of cushioned seats in air-conditioned luxury for just half a dollar in a grand Indian multiplex? A city without Telugu films is a godforsaken place, my Appalraju darling. No jasmines here, only those pathetic surrogates for jasmines; no fragrance of any kind!' Well, we're back in our country. No houses to rent, no state-of-the-art kitchens or sparkling sinks. Daily power cuts for ten hours.

The faucets are always dry. But, you have Simhachalam selling you sampangi flowers at your door, paan cones made of betel leaves, and bottled soda. Today's temperature here is 42°C. I've lost count of the sodas I've downed. Without you, Vizag is a bore. Hurry home to me!

After he'd signed the letter, he went out to check the house number on the front door. 48-12-15. What a quirky number! Four and eight add up to twelve, one and two add up to three. The grand total is fifteen. He wondered if there was anyone other than him who could crack such a complicated code. He was a genius, an intellectual. Anyway, self-adulation is not a virtue, he reminded himself. Srinivasa Ramanujan could decipher such cryptograms in his sleep. Who would win if he, Dr Appalraju, and Ramanujan were locked in a battle of wits? Ramanujan perhaps, he conceded. There are R and J in his name too. Like Ramanujan, he too understood the uniqueness of numbers. An unseen bond existed between him and the world of numbers—once he saw a number he never forgot it.

Well, he'd better write the house number to help his wife to write back. She might write to his office address, God forbid. That was the last thing he wanted. First, he wrote his name with the care of a calligrapher on the envelope. Then he wrote Dwaraka Nagar, Visakhapatnam. Postal code? He couldn't remember. He hadn't paid attention. Oh well, it was not the end of the world. But he'd have to write the house number. What was it? Was it 12-3-15? No, he was not sure. His genius having deserted him, he thought it better to go out again and confirm. For all you know, Srinivasa Ramanujan might have riffled through the books stealthily when Hardy was not around! No shame in taking a second look, he decided.

So, Appalraju went out and checked the door number once again. It was now clear: two ones, one two, one four, one five, one eight. Simple! 48-12-15. He scribbled the number on the envelope.

What next? Find a mailbox. It was eight o'clock. 'Enough time to go to Ooty restaurant for a meal and chuck the letter into the mailbox on the way back,' he calculated. He was not in a mood to change into pants. One could step out of the house in America wearing unpresentable clothes. No one cared. Any rag would do. No questions asked. Why should it be different in India? We just don't try. And what had happened on the one occasion he *did* try? That was the time he'd visited Kakinada to look up his wife's folks. One day, the entire household set out for a drive because it was too stuffy inside the house. He took off his shirt and drove in an undershirt. On the way, his wife, Rani, had spotted a boy selling iced sodas on the sidewalk. She pointed to the soda cart, and cooed into Appalraju's ear, 'I want one, my love.' The dutiful husband that he was, he stopped the cart and asked the soda boy to uncork four iced sodas.

He thought he'd drink one at the cart itself so that he need carry only three cold bottles back to the car. The boy stopped him mid-gulp and yelled, 'What are you doing, man! First take the sodas to your boss and the lady. What impudence! You louts from the countryside are infesting the place and bringing your boorish ways here.' Appalraju couldn't understand why the soda boy took him for a chauffeur. His brother-in-law stepped in hurriedly and said, 'Bava Garu, pass the sodas to me please, I'll take them to my sister.'

The soda boy realized his mistake and turned his ire on Appalraju's brother-in-law, 'What sir, you couldn't buy a decent shirt for your brother-in-law? What happens to the image of our city if our sons-in-law wander the city shirtless?' he said. The vendor didn't know that not only had the young man not bothered to get a respectable shirt for his brother-in-law but had borrowed his Levi's pants instead.

After that experience, Appalraju made up his mind to change the values of this country. Stirred by such reformist zeal, he pulled out from the closet a red undershirt with a pocket but no collar. He thrust a ten-rupee note into the pocket, locked the house, and marched out. He arrived at Emporium Point and flagged down a rickshaw for Ooty restaurant. He got off near a red mailbox and gently slid in the letter to his Queen.

The rickshaw driver shouted after him, 'Sir, you haven't paid the fare!'

'I'm sorry,' Appalraju said and paid him.

Appalraju bought a meal ticket at the restaurant cash register and put the change in his pocket. The food tray arrived and, eating, he slipped into a reverie. Prices in India had shot up into the stratosphere during his stay in America. By the time he'd returned to India, the Janata Party was in power. The Emergency had been lifted. 'It has restored our esteem abroad,' his friends in the USA had argued, sipping whisky. Irritated, he'd asked, 'If India's prestige is so dear to you, why don't you go home and restore it?' The patriotism of these expatriates was limited to boasting about the greatness of their country. They mocked Appalraju for enjoying the comforts of the US even as he criticized the Emergency. He should return to India and protest, they said.

He had returned, but not to protest the Emergency. He wanted to share in the poverty and prosperity of the country, and act on his faith that India was great. Such noble thoughts enriched his meal. By nine o'clock, he had finished his meal, stepped outside the restaurant and bought a betel leaf cone from the paan bunk. As he walked back home, monstrous wall posters warned him in large fonts, 'Naughty Krishna and Cheeky Rama. Hurry up lest you should regret later.' For good measure, at the bottom of the poster blared another admonition 'Delay means Disappointment.'

'I should respect these posters,' he thought. 'The movie seems to have a good cast. I should give it a try. Rani had said she had seen the film in Kakinada and recommended it. I don't even have to get up early. Tomorrow is Sunday, ha!'

He'd passed a theatre on his way to Ooty. His watch showed that he had fifteen minutes to get there. The film had been running for more than 100 days. So, he had no problem getting a ticket. 'Ah, this theatre is air-conditioned,' he chuckled. But the euphoria was short-lived. The management had switched the A/C off. Obviously, they'd not taken a vow at Raj Ghat in Gandhiji's holy presence to keep it running during the entire duration of the movie.

Halfway through the film, Raju got bored and stood up to leave. The audience tried to persuade him to stay, telling him about the fight scenes and dances yet to come. As Raju made his way out, he came between the women and their heroes on the screen. They bristled and cursed him. 'Why should such an impatient man come to see a movie, he should stay at home and not spoil other people's fun!' They yelled at him to sit down.

Raju scurried out of the movie hall and approached the metal gate of the compound. It was locked. The gatekeeper was engrossed in watching the fight scenes from the cheap seats closest to the screen. Raju requested him to come out and open the gate but he said he needed the permission of the manager. 'If you leave the hall in the middle what will the people at the box office think, sir?' the manager chided him.

'This is the last show,' Raju said.

'Last show? There is a morning show in a few hours. People are already lining up because tomorrow is a Sunday. Is it fair of you to leave the hall in their presence?'

Finally, the manager relented and had the gatekeeper open the gate.

Raju stumbled out and wiped the sweat off. He shredded the ticket stub and blew the pieces into the air. Despite everything, he was in a good mood and decided to walk back home. As the old saying goes, the miles go by quickly if we walk with a song on our lips and a hop in our step.

Walking with a jaunty stride, he began belting out, '*Rain drops keep falling on my head...my head....*'

Constable Appalsaami was on patrol. He eyed Raju with suspicion. 'Is this fellow really mad or is he a burglar pretending to be mad?'

He needed to book at least two arrests to keep up with his quota. He took a good look at Raju's flip-flops, the satchel slung across his chest, the red undershirt over a lungi secured by a belt.

'Here's a pickpocket,' he decided.

Appalsaami stopped Raju and asked with mock politeness, 'Where is it raining, sir?'

'My head...my head,' said Raju and stopped singing.

'On your head? Look at the sky and tell me where it is raining from, you drunk.'

'Sergeant, mind your language!' said Raju angrily.

'What, you think I don't know *Ingilis*? I'll thrash you. Where are you coming from at this late hour?'

'From the second show,' Raju said.

'Which movie?'

'*Naughty Krishna and Cheeky Rama.*'

'That show is not over yet.'

'I came away in the middle,' said Raju.

The cop laughed. This was the first time he had heard of anyone walking out from that movie in the middle. Appalsaami saw himself in the role of Naughty Krishna. I certainly look the part, he thought. Wasn't that why he'd been honoured by the theatre owners with the responsibility of being on duty on the opening night?

'Really? You walked out halfway through such a good film?'

'Of course,' said Raju.

'Where's the stub then?'

Raju looked for it in his pocket and remembered that he had thrown it away. Nice touch, the policeman thought.

'Okay, where are you going?'

'Home.'

'Where is it?'

'Dwarakanagar.'

'What's your house number?'

Raju smiled. He was sure he could handle this challenge without a problem, thanks to his special relationship with numbers. There are two ones, one two, one four, one five, one eight.

He thanked Ramanujan and said, '11-24-58.'

'There is no such number in Dwarakanagar,' snapped Appalsaami.

Raju came up with another number. '21-15-84.' He worked it out in his head. Two plus one is three. Five plus one is six. Two times three is six. That is, the sum of the second set of digits is twice the sum of the first set of digits. Now, eight plus four is twelve. Twelve is two times six, the sum of one and five. So, the rule applied to the second and third set of numbers as well. He was thrilled by his own brilliance. That had to be his house number and so he told the policeman.

'Come,' said Appalsaami.

'Where?'

'To the police station.'

'I'm allowed a phone call, according to the rules. You have to produce me before a magistrate if you take me into custody.'

'Will you follow me, or do I have to give you a taste of the baton?'

'Third degree is prohibited by law, officer.'

'Follow me quietly,' the policeman said flourishing his baton. It whipped through the air with a crack like a bullet.

Raju accompanied the policeman docilely to the station.

'What's the matter?' the writer at the station asked.

Raju was shocked that there was nothing like the statutory warning usually heard in American police precincts, the Miranda rights, which warned the suspect that whatever he said could be used against him.

'Caught him prowling around, I think he was planning to burgle a house. Let's put him inside and inform the sub-inspector.'

'I want to make a call and it is your duty to allow me,' Raju asserted his rights.

'You can receive a call, but not make it,' the writer corrected him. 'The guy is firing away in English, man,' he told the constable.

'Who doesn't speak English these days, sir?' Appalsaami said and pushed Appalraju into the lock-up.

That was the last straw.

'I'm Dr Appalraju. You'll regret your actions. There is no Emergency now. The magistrate will take you to task tomorrow. What crime have I committed?' Raju began shouting from behind bars.

'You should inform the SI,' the writer told the constable.

Appalsaami hesitated for an instant, but he walked down anyway to the SI's home, though he feared the boss might resent being disturbed at that late hour.

Luckily for Appalsaami, the SI was awake but in a bad mood. His son had sneaked out to watch a late-night film. He looked up at the cop.

'Not my fault, sir. I just did what you told me to and put the guy in the slammer. He says he will make us pay for this because there is no Emergency. Please tell me what to do.'

The SI told his wife to send his son to the station as soon as he came home from the movie and followed Appalsaami to the station.

'Where is your officer, where's the boss?' Appalraju was shouting when the SI walked in.

'You, there! I'm the boss. What's the problem?' the SI asked.

'Look at the address, sir. All wrong. There is no such number. He was singing that the rain is falling. He claims that he is going home from the theatre but he couldn't even produce the stub,' Appalsaami reeled off an account of what had happened.

'You know you shouldn't go by what a man wears. For that matter, look at what you are wearing. Let me see your ID,' Raju demanded.

The SI was taken aback by this audacity. He'd left home in a hurry, clad in a lungi and banyan.

'In case he acts up,' he told the constable, 'just use the stick.'

Appalsaami made no such attempt because the bars of the lock-up grill got in the way.

'You have no right to torture me. It is for the court to punish me.... Provided I'm guilty,' Raju said.

An orderly interrupted the exchanges. He had a sixteen-year-old boy in tow.

'So, you thought you could do things behind my back and get away with it?' the SI snarled and slapped the boy hard.

The boy began to cry.

'Why is he pummelling the boy? I'll tell his father to file a case, and I'll testify with pleasure!' Appalraju yelled.

'You mean to say our boss can't thrash his own son?' asked the writer.

'Who gave him the right to do that?' Appalraju demanded and bawled out a slogan 'Police violence!'

The boy promptly supplemented, 'Down, down!'

'Where did you find this guy? What a nuisance this bum is, throw him out on the street,' the SI barked.

Once out of the lock-up, Raju asked the SI, 'Do you remember the house number of your relatives in Hyderabad?'

As the SI struggled to answer, his son bolted.

'See, just like you, I too can't remember house numbers...but that doesn't make me a thief,' Raju said and walked out onto the street.

ECLIPSE
BOYA JANGAIAH

The police van took off from the parking lot in Rajahmundry jail. All the police stations on its route to Hyderabad had been alerted. The authorities had received anonymous calls the previous day threatening to ambush the van and spirit away Rajam, the people's poet. The police were ferrying him to Hyderabad for trial on charges of instigating people to challenge the government and trying to destabilize it.

The van arrived at Suryapet after passing through Vijayawada and Kodad on its way. Its progress on the national highway was suddenly blocked by crowds who had amassed at the Ambedkar statue. The police readied their rifles. The officer in charge of the operation stirred uncomfortably when he remembered the anonymous warning.

'Are all these people your followers, sir?' he asked the prisoner and patted his revolver for assurance.

The poet looked up from the pages of the book he was peering into. He moved his gaze towards the police officer, smiled, and glanced at the crowds.

'Driver, turn back and drive down the old road,' barked the officer.

The van changed course, drove down a different road but stopped at the Potti Sriramulu statue in the middle of the town. Here again there were crowds, though not in knots. They were all marching in a single file, shouting slogans. Women in the procession carried empty pots balanced on their heads.

The officer switched on the wireless.

'Hello, hello, police station?'

'Hello, hello, you can proceed; the protesters are on their way to the municipal office to stage a sit-in demanding water. No concern of yours.'

The wireless apparatus went off the line after this brief exercise.

The van continued at the officer's command and raced past Chityala, past Narketpally, and entered Gundrampally.

The place hasn't changed at all, thought Rajam as he surveyed the landscape that flew by on either side of the road. The same tiled houses. One or two new tar-topped roads. A sawmill.

He said to the police officer, 'Sir, the next town is Patangi village. Please stop there for a while. That's my village.'

The police officer didn't want to but remembered that Rajam was a well-known poet. He asked in jest, 'What do you mean by your village, sir? Your village is where you happen to be!'

Rajam contrived a silent smile as a token of appreciation. 'Please pull over for a while,' he said, closing his book and putting it aside.

'Certainly, sir,' said the officer and signalled the driver. The van stopped. Its occupants climbed out.

The road, once far from the town, had now moved close to it. A lot of brushwood had displaced the dense palm grove. Not a trace of the Tangedu bushes on which golden flowers had once blossomed. The poet's head was suddenly flooded with memories of his childhood days.

The crowd that had collected around the van stood and stared at him. None of the townsfolk recognized him, which was understandable, given that the poet was now a man of fifty. Greying stubble, a pair of spectacles in a slim frame. He was a stranger to the children of the town. Young men and women had never seen him. Nor could he recognize anyone.

It was in this village that he'd spent his childhood in fear. It had shattered his family.

'Kavi Garu, it is time to go now,' said the police officer.

Rajam turned around and returned to the van. The rifles followed him and the van started to move again.

Pungent memories! The temple loomed in my mind. My father was one of those drummers that accompany the procession of God's idol, and pick up coins rained on the deity by devotees. We were returning home from one such procession when I stopped and said I'd join him later. I stayed behind near the temple, nebulous questions crowding my young boy's mind.

None of my elders had ever told me what the God in the temple looked like. Even they hadn't seen Him. We couldn't call Him by name. He is always God and not Rama. You couldn't call any Brahmin in the village by name. Call him 'teacher' or 'lord'. Their kids had to be addressed as 'little teacher'. Once when I called the town elder's son by his name, his grandmother looked daggers at me and said, 'How dare you take the name of our child? Call him Little Teacher! You may know how to read a few letters. That doesn't change your caste!' Those were words I couldn't forget.

Barber Yadayya and washerman Pentayya were collecting the extinguished torches tied to the poles of the temporary pavilion near the temple where the procession had culminated. It was almost dark. I'd inched warily towards the pavilion and leaned against one of the poles. I moved close to where the idol was. I was still undetected. If I could just reach the doorway of the sanctum of the temple, I would be able to see Him. I knew that even my grandfather hadn't seen Him, nor had my father. They'd never crossed the road to the side of the temple, let alone dare to enter the pavilion. I must see God. Suppose someone found me? My head grew heavy with these anxieties. Fear rippled through my body.

Suddenly, I felt a strong arm land on my head. My legs trembled and the world blurred. I felt the hand and realized it was not that of the priest. It was a mango branch that had dropped from the

mango festoons strung across the ceiling of the pavilion. The strong urge to see God made me overcome my fright. I took one step after another and reached the threshold and stood there. Sound of footfalls.
I clung to the wall like a lizard and stayed motionless.
The sound was closing in.
My heart beat faster.
My body was drenched in sweat.
It was nobody, just Pentayya and Yadayya. The bundle of new clothes consecrated to God rested on Pentayya's shoulder and the hamper full of cracked coconut sections and fruit was on Yadayya's head. Both of them walked past me, one behind the other. Sighing with relief and thanking God that they had not seen me, I turned to the doorway certain that I could now enter the sanctum. But barring my way was a bronze sceptre, above which emanated a ferocious voice, shouting 'Who is that?' The foot I lifted to step forward withdrew involuntarily. Between me and my eagerness to get a glimpse of God, stood a monstrous figure. My throat became parched. I took flight, and ran all the way back home, without stopping.

Next morning, father, crestfallen, stood facing the town elder in the front yard. Mother crouched behind a neem tree, silently crying. Elders of the other castes crowded around them. I stood beside my father.

The town elder's eyes were aflame. With the end of his dhoti in one hand and the sceptre in the other, he paced restlessly, wearing rustic sandals cobbled by my father. Amma had embroidered them. She and father feared that he might, at any moment, rain blows on them with the very sandals they had made for him.

He looked sharply at us one more time.

He then turned to the assembled elders and asked, 'Did you ever hear of such a thing?'

'Unholy. Inauspicious. Ruin on the village,' said the village priest. He had smeared ash on his forehead, and was wearing a rosary of blackberry beads around his neck and an upper cloth circling his girth.

'Think of a way of pacifying the God,' urged another.

'What pacification? Who will bear the cost?' asked the town elder.

'We still need to buy silks for the priests to conclude yesterday's celebration of God's ceremonial wedding.' The priest's words sounded tired. I didn't know whether it was due to his obese frame or the flurry of festivities or merely his hatred of us.

'So, must we just keep quiet?' the town elder asked.

'What a disaster it is for the village!' said the priest.

'Tell us, what should we do?'

'First, the desecrated temple needs to be whitewashed. We'll deal with the rest later,' said the priest.

'In that case, let's start. Collect the expenses from the boy's father, Eerigadu.'

Father raised his palms in supplication and looked around at the people gathered. Nobody noticed him because everyone stood there with bowed heads. Accosted by apathy, father removed his turban, went down on his knees, and appealed to the people.

'I'm your slave. How can I, without a shirt to cover my body, ever raise the money? You alone can save me.'

It was as if it was not his turban he'd placed on the ground but his head or, perhaps, mine.

'We don't get to eat a square meal a day. Where do we get the money from, my lords? Please take pity on us, you, kind masters. In his ignorance the boy touched the idol.' Hearing these words I stepped back and from behind the tree I could only see my father's folded hands. Hands blackened by hard labour. Hands wearing scratched clay bracelets.

'Take a loan,' said the town elder.

'Who will give me a loan, my lord?' said my father rising to his feet.

'You've a buffalo,' said the priest as if he'd suddenly remembered. 'You can sell it,' the priest said poking a blade of grass with his stick and pointedly looking at it.

'We live on its milk and buttermilk. If we sell it, the boy won't even have the few drops of milk he drinks. We can't live without the buffalo,' said my mother from behind the tree.

The town elder took two steps forward and, pretending to have thought of something, he signalled everyone to close in around him.

'Eeriga, we'll tell you an easy way out. That'll solve the problem.'

My father nodded with downcast eyes.

'My lord, if there is a better solution, what more can I ask for?'

'I know you'll agree. What about your son, will he?'

'He made a mistake. I'll get him to agree. Please let me know.'

'Put him on wage labour and raise a loan against that.'

'Oh, no...I have to go to school,' I said and hid my face in my mother's lap. 'I won't work for wages. I'll study!' I screamed this time.

'Sell the buffalo if the boy doesn't want to work. Luck is not on your side, man. What's left to think about?'—another bit of advice from the other elders present.

Whatever his thoughts, my father bowed, unwound his turban, and tucked it under his arm and asking us to remain behind, hurried home. My mother and I waited under the neem tree. The day was becoming hot. Hushed talk among the gathering continued.

After a while, my father brought the buffalo and its calf and tethered them to the neem trunk. Tears streamed down my mother's cheeks.

Father's sharp looks silenced her just as she was about to say something. She lowered her head and swallowed her grief. Father folded his hands and eyeing everyone assembled said, 'This buffalo is yours.' He didn't stop with that. He said, 'I may starve but I will never suffer a slight.'

No one opened their mouth to help.

Wrenching free of my mother trying to quiet me, I shouted, 'We have no choice! We live on its milk. But you have a choice to purify a temple. At what cost? Does it become defiled just by human touch?'

'Lecturing us, you brat?' the priest asked angrily.

'A village will never prosper without change,' I retorted.

After that incident my parents and I left the village.

⁂

A village is not just made of dwellings. Isn't it also the people who live within it? Mother had muffled my voice then. And now the government has jailed me. But can it stop me from thinking? Can it stop my pen?

The van came to a stop in the plaza of the court. Black robes fluttered on the steps, like the bats that hung upside down from the eaves of the court.

BREEDING MACHINE

SHAIK HUSSAIN SATYAGNI

Remarriage. The mere sound of that word feels like scorpions crawling over my body. I've told Mother several times not to let khalabis, those wretched matchmakers, cross our threshold to market matrimony.

From sunrise to sunset, what do they do? Nothing but go from door to door, wangle coffee at one place, snatch breakfast at another, and wheedle lunch at a third place. What a life! Like parrots, they reel off the virtues of girls waiting to marry. They troll the genealogy of every Muslim family in the town. The good and bad of every household is all grist for their gossip.

Some of them seduce their prey into their web, brandishing attractive nazaranas, gifts, and singing panegyrics about their clients' marriageable children. The khalabis exaggerate their clients' wealth. 'You're lucky to bag such a match,' they whisper into the ears of the boys' parents. 'It's your good fortune that your girl is stepping into that household,' they tell the girls' side.

Lately, Rabia khalabi has been dropping in at our house quite frequently. Never mind that there is no girl of marriageable age at home. My three brothers are already married, two of them with the good offices of this garrulous woman. One day, I heard her chirping in my mother's ears that it is a good idea to look for a husband for me.

'The boy has been widowed recently. Poor guy, he is struggling to bring up motherless children. He has a government job that brings him a comfortable salary. He's pressing me to find him a good girl,' she was telling my mother when I entered the room and surprised them. They instantly changed the topic, conspiring to put the real topic on hold.

Thereafter, my heart always palpitated wildly at her sight. I felt as if there was a fireball hovering over my head and counted the minutes for her to disappear. I'd regain my peace of mind only after her exit.

Rabia came again today, maybe to reopen the old conversation with my mother. What kind of disaster awaited me, I wondered. Though I pretended to browse a book, my mind was busy with thoughts of my mother and the khalabi. I tuned my antenna to pick up on their conversation. The words on the page didn't register in my brain. I was afraid they'd call for me every time I heard them raise their voices. But it passed.

Father returned from afternoon prayers. It was a Friday; so, he didn't go to his shop, the biggest in town. It was named Sultana Cut Piece Centre, after me.

'I've asked the boy's side to come see Sultana,' my mother told him after he sat beside her on the mat.

He looked at her pensively.

'It has been three months since the iddat—the wait period after her separation from her husband—has lapsed. Age is catching up with her. We can't sit tight. How long can she stay with us? We can provide all comforts but not a husband. I never thought Allah would deny His blessings to our only daughter.' Tears flowed from my mother's eyes. She stuffed her mouth with her sari to stifle her sobs.

'Quiet, Salima. Whatever Allah desires will happen. Is it in our hands to escape what He determines is our lot? I've been praying to Him at every namaz to rekindle the light in my child's life. He is merciful and will certainly shower His blessings on her.'

I was convinced that Father had endorsed my mother's plans. Their conversation upset me. I ran to my room.

After the evening prayers I lay on my bed. Mother has been

urging me not to go to sleep without dinner. 'I'm not hungry,' I said. She wouldn't listen. I drank a glass of milk to escape her nagging.

However hard I tried, I couldn't fall asleep. My mind had surrendered to the buzz of indecipherable thoughts. How was my baby, Rizwana? She wouldn't fall asleep unless she'd played on my chest and gurgled 'Ammi, Ammi' and patted my cheeks. She would kiss me and refuse to go to her father despite his pleas. Nothing could happen in the house unless she had fallen asleep.

All my woes began after Rizwana's birth. In the first seven years of our marriage, life had been full of celebration for us. We sought each other out. Raja Khan was sometimes uncomfortable talking to me because I had a B. A. while he had not even cleared his Intermediate exams.

His father owned a big jewellery shop in town. Raja had taken over the business after his father's death. In managing the business, he'd surpassed his father quickly. Father had arranged my marriage with Raja because Raja Khan's father had been his friend. Raja was burly, with a squashed nose. Yet, his was a face that drew people in.

My parents had given in dowry whatever Raja's mother had demanded. My mother-in-law was gentle and treated me as if I was her daughter. Raja was quite proud of me, my beauty. He'd write lyrics about me like a poet. Life was good, but not for long. As if by ill luck, my first child died when she was two. And then I had three more daughters.

All the love notwithstanding, Raja divorced me one fine morning. He uttered 'talaq' three times. What did I do to deserve such harsh punishment? Was it my fault that I had given birth to three daughters?

'Three daughters in a row! I hoped the third would be a son. Now the whole town makes fun of me. I can't step out of my house and hold my head up high,' he'd constantly complain.

Discontent simmered. I'd told him to take a second wife if he really wanted a boy. Two wives would be too many to manage, he'd said. Not wanting a showdown, I'd tolerated every taunt of his. But one day, like a bolt from the blue, he came home with two witnesses and shouted 'talaq, talaq, talaq'. That was the end.

The community elders met and demanded that he return the gold he'd been given at the time of our marriage. His relatives argued that with three girls to raise, it was not possible. In the end, he yielded to the pressure and agreed to return the gold. The elders told me to accept the money and go home. I meekly accepted their verdict.

In ten minutes, the curtain had come down on ten years of marriage. Raja Khan had turned me into a childbearing machine. And now, my mother wants to hand over the machine to a different person. I am overcome with self-pity at my helplessness. I have been crying myself to sleep lately, and I do the same tonight.

Next morning, as usual, I sit down on the threshold of my house at the trunk road intersection. My children, who are no more mine, now tramp to the convent school every day at eight, and pass in front of our house. The convent is in a lane right next to our house. I'm afraid that they will lose their way if I don't keep a watch over them. I don't skip this routine, ever. Every day I wait for the eight o'clock bell expectantly. Would Raja Khan scold them for talking to me? My heart dims. I am angry with myself for entertaining such negative thoughts. Those ten minutes I spend with my children are my anodyne. Bliss. All my pain vanishes whenever I hug them. This wait, sitting on the threshold, is for savouring that moment of joy.

They're my children who experienced the warmth of my womb for nine months. Today, I can't even say they're mine. They're Raja Khan's children. Not mine.

Lo, they're coming. I feel as if paradise is moving towards me.

'Ammi jaan!' they chorus together and fall in my lap. I crane my neck to see if any of Raja Khan's men are snooping around. The children twist around me. I give them milk candy but the youngest refuses to touch it and pouts.

'Won't you eat, Rizwana?' I say.

She shakes her head.

'Why?'

Her eyes fill. 'Mother beat me,' she sobs, looking at me piteously. I feel a stabbing in my heart. Mother is Raja Khan's new wife of ten days.

'Why?' I ask the eldest.

'Rizzoo insisted on sleeping by the new auntie's side when daddy and the new auntie were in their bed. Auntie brought her to my bed. But Rizzoo went back to their room. Auntie lost her temper and slapped her.'

Her words rent my heart. My children are motherless while I'm still alive.

'Didn't your daddy say anything?'

'No,' the elder children say.

'Keep her with you, Ammi. She has been crying all night. She stopped only after daddy said he would throw her out of the house.'

My second daughter was about to say something. I shut her mouth with my hand.

My mother, who heard the children crying, comes out and says, 'If you coddle them, they'll never leave you. You must harden your heart and forget them.'

The three hang on to the skirts of their grandmother. 'Daddy will beat you if he finds out you were here. Go away,' says my mother and sends all of them out. She then turns away from me and blots her eyes. Seeing them leave, I can't contain myself either.

One evening, Father came home in a frenzy. Seeing me in the hallway, he said, 'What, you're not ready yet?'

I understood what he meant but said nothing.

'They're coming in the evening. Make yourself presentable.'

I looked into his eyes.

'You don't understand, my child. Do as we tell you,' he said and caressed my head. I built up the courage to say, 'Excuse me, Father, but I don't want to marry.'

'My child, it is our tradition.'

'I don't deny that. But our scriptures don't sanction talaq, yet it has become a game. You know, Father, what's the real purpose of talaq?

'Only when man and wife are unhappy with each other; when it becomes difficult to carry on as a couple; when there are no chances of rapprochement and when they think it is impossible to go any further, only then talaq is permitted. Just uttering talaq three times on petty pretexts is not fair, Father.'

He nodded and gazed at me thoughtfully.

'Look, Razia Sultana, it is their sin, not yours. You're an educated woman. We won't force anything on you against your wishes. But make sure you don't bring shame upon us,' Father said.

Mother walked on to the scene and seemed to understand what was going on at once. 'We don't want anything other than your happiness,' she said.

'People like me who married fools can't escape this fate. But I want to lend a helping hand to unfortunate women who are trapped in such awful situations. I want to teach a lesson to irresponsible men like Raja Khan. Tomorrow, I will apply to a college to study law. I want to be a lawyer and take on such talaq abusers. Please, give me a chance,' I pleaded.

'My child....' They stop mid-sentence, too happy for words.

'I'll prove that your daughter is virtuous. I'll make sure that the family reputation doesn't suffer. Please bless me,' I said, touching their feet.

'May Allah protect you,' they blessed me by placing their hands on my head. 'Your happiness is our happiness,' they said, together.

WATER

BANDI NARAYANASWAMI

Dawn. The alarm, set for five, goes off. My wife is startled as if woken from a nightmare. She involuntarily shushes the alarm. I'm a typist at Hirehal Mandal. Unless breakfast and a four-tier lunch box are ready by eight, I can't board the bus that takes me to Hirehal. This daily deadline sets my wife's nerves on edge.

'Water! Water! Water's been turned on, sister,' cries our neighbour Venkatesulu, drumming on the door. Sounds of disorganized commotion seep in from the outside. My wife darts out as if she has won the lottery. She hears Venkatesulu sprinting to the municipal tap. The clanging of brass containers fills the air.

'Get up, get up. Get the mosquito curtain out of my way. Water's flowing again. Keep an eye on the children,' my wife shouts a series of commands. She scurries to the kitchen, picks up two pitchers, and exits with one under each arm.

I'm groggy and anxious, not about the boy but the one-year-old who, if she were to wake, would raise hell. She doesn't trust anyone except her mother, and will shriek like a factory siren if her mother is out of sight.

I yank aside the mosquito curtain and stretch out next to the children. I'd closed my eyes for hardly ten minutes, when I feel the rumblings of nature's call. We share a septic latrine with our neighbours. My wife and our neighbour's wife, take turns filling a plastic bucket with water for washing. Each hopes the other will fill it. Who is generous enough to spare two pitchers of water during this drought?

I open the latrine door and take a peek inside the bucket. Empty. There's no water. I sneak into the kitchen to steal some water. Suddenly, my wife appears and screams her heart out, as if a great calamity has befallen us, 'Don't touch that! That's drinking water. Take the hard water from the plastic pitcher next to it.'

I return from the latrine and find she has already swept and washed the front yard and is ready to make another run to the municipal tap. She says, 'We have to wait for our turn if we don't save our place in the line.'

The baby wakes up and proceeds, in no time, from a whimper to an unbridled wail.

'Oh, I'm trapped now! She won't let go of me if she sees me. Please keep an eye on her. I'll check the queue and bring some water,' my wife whispers into my ear, hiding behind the wall, trying to sneak out without the little devil noticing.

I panic. 'No, no! She won't stay with me. Take her with you. Otherwise she'll cry her head off.'

Poor woman. Convinced that there is no escape, she lifts the child into the crook of her arm and asks with an entreating face, 'Okay, will you take a shower and bathe the boy when he is up?'

I'd have shouted at her for passing on the job of bathing the boy to me, were it not for that piteous look. She toils away the whole day, keeping watch on the municipal tap for any hint of water. I know that she'd never let me do a single chore if it were not for the water runaround. Poor thing, it is not as if she has four arms and four legs to haul water and run the house too, all by herself.

I enter the bathroom and find she has kept the hot water ready for my bath. Not more than three or four small mugfuls, though. Can't help it, I have to make do with what's available. When I was an M. A. student in Waltair, hostelers stood outside the bathroom and shouted, 'Enough, come out,' as I went on dousing myself with mug after mug of hot water. I enjoyed the evening baths even more, with no one around to hustle me. That was the Golden Age.

I remember, my mother often complained in playful anger, 'I'll die one day hauling water for you, my boy.' Poor woman died before there was running water at her house. How happy she would have been to see this day! But in Rayadurg, where we live, it's no simple matter even for those who have a tap at home. Water is a matter of luck, trickling out of the tap whimsically.

'If we want to move to a house with a tap, the rent is not one, or two, but a whole four hundred rupees. What's left then to feed or clothe ourselves? And, there's no guaranteed supply in this town even if you have a tap,' my wife always says. Hell, from dawn to dusk it's a constant scramble for water. Entrusting the child to someone, my wife returns with a pitcher on her left shoulder and another tucked under her armpit and spits out, 'Come quick, help me lower this.' I snatch the pitcher irritably from her and vengefully bang it down in the bathroom.

Unmindful of my mood, she cries, 'Lower it gently! Don't dent the pitcher.' She dumps the two vessels in the kitchen and takes out two empty ones, ready to go out again and bring more water. The boy shouts from the latrine, 'I need water, Amma.'

My wife helps the boy wash and tells him, 'Get your father to bathe you. Go to school and come back for lunch.' She disappears again to get water.

It is nearly eight by the time she finishes a second round of hauling water. The boy has left for school, which opens its gates at half past seven. I come home after a short walk and am happy to smoke a cigarette after tea. It moves me to see my wife stepping in with the child in one arm and the water-filled vessel in another. I move forward and relieve her of the weeping child but the brat lurches towards her mother, hands outstretched, and revs up the pitch.

'What a monster of a child! Won't stay with anyone. What am I to do, carry the water or this bundle?' my wife bristles at the child and raises her voice, 'Will you shut up, you devil?'

She then flops on the bed complaining of exhaustion. The child crawls onto her mother's bosom, crying even more at being dumped on the bed.

'Poor child is hungry perhaps. She is crying because you haven't fed her since morning,' I tell her gently. I detect tears under her eyelids that are closed with tiredness. I go into the kitchen, prepare milk with Amul powder in a feeding bottle, and bring it to her.

'With this water headache, it is difficult to take care of the child. I want to send her to my mother,' she says blotting her eyes.

'Okay,' I say.

She takes the child off her chest and feeds her the Amul milk.

'There is no time to cook now. Please eat lunch at a restaurant,' she says.

Though I say okay, I'm not sure I want to eat out. Restaurant food turns my stomach, and I invariably get amoebiasis. She knows this but what can she do! She takes my hands and presses them to her eyes with love.

A few days later, I come home around nine in the evening with a friend, who happens to be in Rayadurg on election duty. He is to stay with us. I find that there is not a drop of water at home.

My wife borrows two mugs of drinking water from the neighbour and serves us.

'Please don't get me wrong. There is no water for a shower,' I say to my friend next day. 'But, there is enough for a quick wash. Why don't you stay for lunch?' The words slip from my lips but my friend is ready to leave.

'Some other time, brother. I must go now,' my friend says and leaves, understanding our predicament.

After my friend leaves, my wife says, 'I'm worried about our daughter.'

'She must be happier there,' I say.

'I think of her all the time, I want to see her,' says my wife and sheds tears.

It's not even been a week since the child had left home.

'I can't bear to hear those petty people say all kinds of things at the water tap. I cannot deal with them. Please ask for a transfer out of here,' she pleads, wiping her eyes.

Is my father-in-law a minister that I can wangle a transfer at will?

The next day, like every other day, I rise at dawn, but find that there is no water to wash my face. The pump near our house is out of order. My wife brings water from the neighbour's house.

There is a stream ten miles away that supplies water to Rayadurg municipality. Two pumps set four miles apart force the water towards the town. Water stops flowing when there is load shedding or power failure. If the motor conks, there is no water for three or four days.

Naidu's opposition party rages at the municipal chairman Ram Reddy for luring voters with a promise to resolve the water problem but once elected, doing nothing about it. Naidu's men smash the water pipes. The town goes without water. People gripe that Reddy has swallowed municipal money by installing second-hand motors. Others gossip that he cuts off water to opposition areas.

Water politics. The politics of stealing votes. The politics of swindling.

No water the next day as well.

'Get a vesselful from the fort,' says my wife.

'What, me? Carry vessels?' I ask her, surprised.

'I can't walk that far.'

'Stumble down the road like a coolie carrying water? Don't ask me to do such things,' I say firmly.

Wouldn't it be nice if someone could find a way to cook without water!

'We'll get food from the outside today,' I tell my wife.

'What about water to drink?'

'Borrow. You and the junior can manage with it. I'll go out and fend for myself,' I say.

She loses her patience and screams.

I turn a deaf ear and slip out.

'Women allow men to have the upper hand in the beginning and slowly over time learn to order them around,' I think bitterly. 'No matter what, I won't touch a single pitcher today.' I decide to remain firm.

I return home at eight in the night. The boy is playing outside the house. The house is silent. My wife acts distant.

I can't get myself to ask her if she has made dinner.

'Give me the carry-out dinner box. I'll pick up some food from a restaurant,' I say awkwardly.

'Dinner is ready. There's water in the jug. Wash your hands and sit down for dinner,' my wife says and calls the boy to join.

'Oh, there's water to wash?' I lack the courage to ask her how she has managed to get the water.

She spreads the mat and serves food in three plates. She places two jugs of water. 'One for drinking and the other for washing your hands,' she cautions us.

I feel guilty and imagine what pains she must have gone through to get this water.

My silence, her reticence, and my effort to get her to talk are all awkward. I'm uneasy.

Junior is talking about his teacher with great animation. My wife and I join him in conversation and, soon, we get talking to each other. The fellow finishes his dinner and washes his hands over the plate. When my wife takes a look at his plate, she is shocked. The plate is overflowing and he is still at it.

'Don't waste water,' she yells.

He is scared and stops playing with the water. She notices that it is the big jug and that he has emptied the water meant for drinking. 'Good heavens,' she cries and thrashes the boy.

'No, Amma. I won't do it again,' he wails loudly. Seeing him in tears, I become emotional. She continues with her rampage. I try to stop it.

She suddenly stops beating him and bursts into tears. The boy stands behind me clinging to my neck. I calm everyone down.

It's ten o'clock. I'm preparing to go to bed. Suddenly, cries of 'water, water' rise from the street. I pick up two pitchers and step out. 'I'll join you,' I tell her.

She's been pestering me for a week to go out and help her bring water. Now when I'm ready to do so, she is struck by guilt that she is making her husband haul water.

I kiss the sleeping boy, carry him to the neighbour's place and leave him there, and join my wife.

Knots of people swarm the tap near our house.

Cries, shouts, vessels roped to bicycles.

Harmless commotion.

Some women sample the water and send the word around that it really is drinking water. Sometimes hard water is piped in from a different stream.

My wife asks if the water is pouring or dripping.

'Yes, like a child piddling,' says someone.

We migrate to another tap near the bus stand, even if it is a bit far away. Crowds greet us there too.

'It's better here, the flow I mean,' confirms my wife.

The municipal tap is sandwiched between a bus stand and a hotel. Cinema posters are pasted on walls that surround the urine-soaked ground, an acrid smell radiating from it. Rotten fruit jettisoned by fruit stalls ferment and attract cattle that stand whisking their tails and foraging in the mess. Clouds of flies levitate around the mounds of fruit garbage. Women are chatting, covering their noses with the ends of their saris. Shops and eating places are shuttered. But a sprinkling of people is loitering near the paan shop and around the teacart illuminated by a petromax light.

'Oh, not here,' says my wife when I ask her if she wants tea. I drink tea, smoke a cigarette, and saunter around. I fail to connect with the other men there.

Jokes about Rayalaseema district make the rounds.

'Anantapuram will become a desert after a few years.'

'Then we'll travel by camels to visit each other.' Laughter.

'Cyclones are drowning towns everywhere. Here in Anantapuram, there is not even a drop of rain. Even if a deluge were to sink the world, we'll be safe. Our Rayalaseema will be safe and afloat.'

I feel sleepy and yawn. All other eyes are riveted to the vessel under the tap.

The metallic sound of water falling into the empty vessel is very annoying. I pray for each vessel to fill up soon. But others are amused by the sound of water at different stages of filling. They are counting the number of people ahead of them, hoping that their turn will come soon.

'Sister, my husband has just got off the truck and is in the middle of his meal. There is not a drop of water at home. Please let me fill one pitcher,' a woman is pleading, trying to jump the queue.

Suddenly, a dog comes by and dips its snout into a pitcher full of water.

'My god, the dog has touched the water,' cry the water seekers and shoo the animal away.

One middle-aged maid stops the owner from emptying the dog-touched vessel and says, 'Why do you waste water? Pour it into my vessel. It will be useful at least to wash hands.'

The paan shop has closed. The teacart has left. It is midnight and finally our turn.

My wife places four vessels promptly near the tap afraid someone might grab our place.

But her fears turn out to be unfounded.

As my wife pushes our vessel under the tap and sighs in relief, the water stops dripping.

'Oh, good heavens, the electricity is out. What will we do?' Everyone is worried. My wife looks like someone has snatched her dinner from her before she can start to eat. A new fear: will there be someone to switch on the pump when the electricity comes back?

It's all in the hands of God.

The electricity comes back on, and joy erupts, like in a movie theatre when the power is back after a half-hour breakdown. Five minutes later, water gushes out of the tap.

My wife is about to push her vessel under the water when an old woman pleads to let her fill just one vessel. My wife says no and the old woman at once raises her voice and says, 'If everyone brings three or four vessels when will we get our turn? Fill one of yours and give us a chance.'

Soon there are two shouting groups: owners of four or six vessels on one side and the labourers with just one or two pots on the other.

'Unlike you, we can't manage with one or two vessels,' a woman pitches in.

'You mean I am a stupid old woman, a dirty old woman, a scrappy old woman, and that I need only one pitcher, whereas you need six vessels and the one above your station needs sixty vessels? Each according to their status! Status determines one's needs. Who are you, madwoman, to tell us to ration our needs? Is that what you are saying to me?'

My wife peers into my face, concerned that the words of the old woman might hurt me.

When I try to lift one vessel on to my shoulder my wife stops me saying, 'Don't do that. You just accompany me home.' She tucks one vessel under her armpit and transfers another on to her shoulder. She leaves, telling someone to keep a watch on her vessels as they fill, till she comes back again. I snatch one of the vessels from her when we turn into our street and tell her, 'It's okay. Nobody will notice us in the dark. Our prestige will not suffer.'

There is a lot of laughter and mirth in the neighbourhood when they hear that we are going to Anantapuram to celebrate Ugadi. 'Lucky people, enjoy. You will save yourself from the water headaches…at least for a week.' Though the Brahmaputra and Ganga don't flow through Anantapuram, it will certainly be better. My wife always goes gaga over the tap her parents have at their house in Anantapuram.

'How is the water position there?' she asks visitors from Rayadurg while we are in Anantapuram.

'Don't ask. You're lucky to be here—there's been no water there for the last four days,' they tell her. My wife sighs in relief as if she has escaped a disastrous accident by a whisker.

Rayalaseema's water problems are in the news. The people lambast the ruling party for the water famine, undertake fasts unto death, and, in the end, start bargaining for party tickets, office perks. Some silently join the ruling party.

My vacation is over. There is a lot of commotion in the air when we return to Rayadurg because the vandals who had damaged the water pipelines have been rounded up and jailed. Municipal chairman Ram Reddy claims that they belong to Naidu's party. But Naidu retorts, 'They're not my men. You can check with them.'

The municipality now installs water meters in every house, rations water, and collects a penalty from whoever exceeds the limit. Secret meetings are held where people ask, 'But why are no meters installed in the houses of people of Chairman Ram Reddy's caste?'

There is fracas at the tap on the evening of our return from Anantapuram. A clash between two women ends up as an all-out war between their men.

The police drag the two men to the police station, 'Come on, you bastards, march to the station. You don't know how to be civilized. You shouldn't stay in this town.'

The two women follow them crying and abusing each other all the way to the station.

Next morning, the four real culprits who broke the pipes are freed from custody, unscathed, and strut around town. They glow with pride, basking in their power and influence. The town is awash with rumours that an unseen political hand has arranged their release.

The two 'uncivilized men' are still rotting away in custody after three days because they and the police cannot agree on the amount needed to buy their release.

There's a saying that it is possible to tell how civilized a person is by the way they use water. But how can people who do not have access to a single pot of water ever dream of civilization?

PREDATORS
SYED SALEEM

Kotesu parked himself near the Ryves Canal lock, with his neck outstretched like a vulture eyeing carrion. His eyes travelled down the stream to study the shadows playing on the water not far from him. 'There is something odd about the blend of colours,' he thought. The red object moving seductively in his direction looked at first sight like a wet, unfurled sari. Shielding his eyes against the sun, he squinted into the waters and saw that it really was a red sari.

He stood on the high embankment of the canal, his humble frame filled with hope. His hawkish eyes glowed with expectation. He was sure his two-hour wait had paid off. Kotesu watched his reward approach the gates. An answer to his prayers. His eyes combed the surroundings anxiously for spoilsports who could cheat him of his catch. The couple of people he spotted moping around hardly noticed him. Others that passed by mistook him, with his tatters, emaciated cheeks and gaunt face, for a beggar. They filed past unconcerned.

'Is begging heinous?' he wondered. Is rifling through the bodies of dead strangers a crime? How can you call it stealing, when the corpses neither forbade nor approved such a crime? He'd never used force. Some loathsome human dregs he knew exhumed bodies, rid them of clothes and jewellery, and then sold the items. In his view, he was better than such guttersnipes. The poor wretches that jumped into the river to kill themselves did so of their free will. He had not driven them to suicide. He always waited for the bodies to float down from the Krishna River and get to the locks near the Ryves Canal masonry bridge. Only then did he rob them of gold ornaments. 'It is a wretched life nevertheless,' he conceded.

It had been like this, despicable, since he could remember: hunger, penury, indignity, disease, and hell. Images of his father coming home drunk and battering his mother daily had made him resolve to never touch alcohol. That resolve had melted away even before he'd shed adolescence. He loafed about the streets, watched blue films in Leela Mahal, and smoked bidis.

His happiness at the death of a feral father was short-lived. It had heaped additional misery on him. His mother, who had, until now, turned a blind eye to his vagrant ways, began badgering him to go out and bring home some money. After one such maternal dressing-down, he'd repaired to the canal to sulk. The sulk ended when he saw the body of a woman bobbing up near the canal gates. His eyes lit up when he saw the glittering mangalasutram, the sacred wedding chain, around her neck. A second look revealed an additional slender gold chain. Kotesu had realized in an instant that if he wavered, someone else, perhaps a policeman, would do it. Without a second thought he'd jumped into the water and briskly gathered the gold on the body.

He had sold off the loot to a pawnbroker, soaked himself in liquor, eaten chicken biryani in Srinivasa Hotel, and then gone home to sleep. His rest was disturbed—he'd been plagued by nightmares of the dead woman coming back to life and laughing at him viciously. She'd opened her eyes just as he snatched away the ornaments, sailed into his hut, and demanded her things back.

For a whole month, the nightmare had held him back from the locks. But the hardships of life had preyed upon him like a blood-sucking vampire and driven him back to his scavenging ways. After a month of restraint, Kotesu had reappeared at the canal site.

Now, he had learned to concentrate his five senses on the gold, like Arjuna, the legendary archer from the Mahabharata, fixing his aim on the bird's eye. His nose no longer flinched at the stench of the passing cadavers. Their touch no more sent a shudder through his body. For him, to lift the gold off the bodies became child's play, as easy as pulling it off a peg. He braced himself as he saw a bloated red sari sailing towards him. 'No hurry, the body will stop at the gates anyway,' he calculated. He would dive in and finish the job as adroitly as he could catch fish.

He was afraid that fucker Narigadu might be lurking somewhere close by to swoop down on the treasure. His eyes surveyed the scene for Narigadu who, in his eyes, was a menace. Kotesu had ruled the roost for eight months. Ever since Narigadu appeared, he'd literally snatched the food off his plate. The guy was older and stronger. Kotesu knew he could never win if it came down to a fight. Narigadu had already bested him four or five times.

He looked around once again and was convinced that it was not prudent to wait for the body to reach him. Yet, Kotesu had to abandon the dive because Narigadu had appeared out of nowhere and leapt into the water, and was now rapidly closing the distance between him and the woman's body.

Kotesu raged impotently at Narigadu. Like hunger, his anger singed his innards. His feeble heart beat weakly, eager to clobber his rival. 'Don't get in my way, just this once. I promise, you won't see me here for another month. Let it be my turn this time. Spare me for the sake of my sister. Her husband has deserted her for failing to bring in the five hundred rupees we owe him. I can't bear to see sorrow darken her eyes. Just five hundred rupees will do, not to drink or visit brothels but to make my sister happy once again. Her marriage, worth a mere five hundred rupees, must be saved,' he beseeched Narigadu in his mind.

Narigadu was within reach of his prize now. It was then that Kotesu's eyes lit up once again, after he'd despondently gazed at the red sari that had slipped from his hand. He took a second look. After walking a few steps along the embankment, he paused and gazed at what was happening.

Kotesu saw the red sari trapped in Narigadu's hands—but where was the corpse? Narigadu must have thought the sari had disengaged itself from the body. He had swum back and was searching for the corpse. He went under the water and surfaced three times, his head covered with flotsam. Not a hint of the body.

Narigadu's discomfiture set Kotesu laughing wildly. Kotesu told Narigadu, who was glaring at him, 'Keep all the gold to yourself,' and continued to laugh.

'Stay there if you have guts...you're destined to die by my hands today,' snarled Narigadu, swimming back to the embankment. Ready to flee before Narigadu reached the shore, Kotesu said from the embankment, 'Okay, come up. We will see who lives and who dies.'

Narigadu went up the embankment but whirled back in terror. Kotesu was baffled. What scared him? As if in answer, a heavy hand fell on his shoulder with a thud. It belonged to a policeman guffawing like an apparition. Kotesu knew the punk. 'This fellow is worse. If I feed off cadavers, this guy swipes commission from the likes of us,' he muttered under his breath.

'Rascal, what are you up to?' the policeman asked.

'Nothing, sir. Just passing time.'

'Shut up, you son of a whore. You think I can't see through your games? You think I'm a fool to believe you're here to appreciate nature or breathe in the fresh air? I'll skin you alive. Take out whatever you have, you parasite,' the policeman said, hitting Kotesu on the knees with his baton.

'I beseech you, sir. I swear I didn't even get into the water. That fellow saw the body first. See, how dry my shirt is?' Kotesu pulled his shirt forward for the policeman to see.

'You, clod, you think you're very smart. Don't play games with me. I'm sure the two of you are in league. Don't think you can cheat me out of my share.'

Clenching Kotesu's shirt with his left hand, the cop reached for Narigadu and shouted, 'Do you need a special invitation? Will you come out of the water or wait until you get a taste of this baton?'

Narigadu crawled up to the cop trembling with fear and wringing the water from his clothes.

'Where is the loot? Shell it out,' the policeman barked.

'I haven't taken anything, sir,' said Narigadu meekly, like a tiger morphed into a cat.

'You think the corpse is your mother's property? Take it out! I have other things to do.'

'What corpse, sir? Do you see it here? It's just the sari. I swear on my mother, sir.'

The policeman took a sharp look at the sari.

'Rascal! Tell me, what happened to the body?'

'No body, sir. Only the sari.'

The policeman landed one good whack on Narigadu's back.

'I'll charge you with murder. Put you in the cooler. Tell me, where's the body and what happened to the gold jewels?' the policeman said shifting his hand from Kotesu's shirt to Narigadu's collar.

Kotesu thought it might be a good time to wriggle out. He said, 'Sir, may I go now?'

'Where are you going, bastard? Aren't you both in cahoots? First empty your pockets!'

The policeman shoved his hand into Kotesu's pocket and searched. He found a beedi stub, two one-rupee coins, a half-rupee coin, and a soiled five-rupee note. He stuffed the loot into his pocket and said, 'You may go now. I'll settle this fellow's account.'

He turned to Narigadu and asked, 'Now tell me, where is the corpse and where are the things you took from it?' He then used the baton on him.

The policeman saw Kotesu still hanging about and asked him, 'What are you around waiting for? Do you want me to work the baton on you?'

'Sir, I haven't had a drop of water since morning. I'm hungry, please give me some money.'

'What money? You mean your hard-earned cash? Bloody thief, get lost without making a fuss.'

'Sir, true, it is a wretched way to make money. But hunger is no less wretched. I've nothing to buy tea with, sir. Please return my money,' Kotesu begged.

'Chee, useless fellow. You're all parasites. Take this and perish,' the policeman flung two and a half rupees at him.

Kotesu wanted to stand around and enjoy what awaited Narigadu but was afraid that if he stayed on too long the policeman might change his mind and take his money back. He left the scene at a brisk pace.

When he was out of the policeman's sight he slowed down. Two one-rupee coins and a half-rupee coin. 'Shit, what a miserable life...a policeman calls me a parasite,' Kotesu hated himself and spat in disgust. 'I'm not just a parasite but the vermin that thrive on shit. But what about the policemen who suck the blood of vermin like us? What about the officials who open the locks and push the bodies into the jurisdiction of Guntur police to avoid the bother of conducting an investigation, and the expense of performing the last rites for these unclaimed bodies?'

To escape the pain of these questions, he reignited the bidi stub and filled his lungs with smoke. Ah, some relief! The sky was overcast. A gentle breeze hinted at rain. It was a disappointing day. He would have to go home and listen to his mother's curses, look at the piteous face of his sister waiting to see if he'd brought the money for her dowry. How was he to console her?

Kotesu's melancholy abruptly lifted when he remembered his defeat from last month and today's avenging humiliation of Narigadu, blow for blow, insult for insult, and sneer for sneer.

That day a month ago, it was Narigadu who had first seen the body floating down. When he ran to jump into the canal Kotesu had tripped him and felled him to the ground. Narigadu rose to his feet and landed a couple of blows on Kotesu's face. Kotesu was dazed and his nose began to bleed. He kicked Narigadu hard in the stomach. As Kotesu tried to flee towards the canal, Narigadu stood in the way. Kotesu dug his teeth into Narigadu's right hand. In pain, Narigadu pushed Kotesu just as he neared the water.

'I can make it if I leap into the canal, swim like mad, and rip the mangalasutram and earrings off the body, then race to the other embankment,' Kotesu had thought. He'd dove into the water but in a blink, Narigadu had jumped in too. Kotesu swam faster than him and reached the body, its face turned towards the gates. It had a string with a pendant of turmeric root around its neck. Hoping to find a gold mangalasutram, he turned the body towards him. It was the madwoman that begged for money on their street. He had turned to look behind him and seen Narigadu laughing wildly.

'The body is full of gold. Take it all. I won't ask for a share,' Narigadu had been in stitches.

Today, after one month, Kotesu was happy that Narigadu had finally got his due. How should he celebrate? Radhabai or booze? Which would give him a high—the nectar that burns the throat or sex that exhilarates the body? He chose Radhabai.

He found her sitting on her haunches in front of her hut, barbequing kebabs. Her shining thighs and taut body were a treat. She took time off from barbequing to get into bed with the client waiting inside her hut for five rupees. Once the client left, she returned and spoke to Kotesu.

'You want some kebabs?'

'Let's go to your shack,' he stammered, unable to look into her intoxicating eyes.

'The rate is ten rupees.'

'It was five rupees four days ago?'

'I hiked the rates. Haven't the others done it? You pay others without a murmur but you want to haggle with me. Get out of my sight,' she said.

'That is too much. I'm an old client. Give me a concession,

Radhabai,' Kotesu pleaded.

'Do you get a concession at the liquor store? Nothing less than ten rupees will do,' Radhabai said stubbornly.

'Okay, let's walk in.'

'Pay first.'

Kotesu grumbled and took out the two and half rupees from his pocket and pressed it into the hooker's palm.

'The rest on credit,' he said.

Radhabai considered the stuff in her hand with disdain.

'You wretched bum, put this money on your pyre! You want to roll in my bed like a pig without a dime in your pocket? Go to hell,' she said and threw the money in his face.

He picked up the money from the floor and muttered, 'You fatty...sleeping with you is like mating with a hog.'

The liquor shop gave him credit. He drank with a vengeance. Drank because the policeman had called him a parasite. Drank because Radhabai had said he was a pig. Drank because it was a day when nobody jumped into the Krishna to die. Drank because he remembered his mother. Drank because his sister waited with her big, black eyes to get the money to pay the needed dowry and reunite with her husband.

He awoke to the sound of his mother's voice unfolding a catalogue of his misdeeds.

'Is there anything that you do other than drink and loll in bed? It's been more than three months since that rascal ditched your sister. She cries every day. I'm able to feed her with what little I get working in four homes. You don't have the sense to send the girl to her husband's place. Lazing in the bed is all you do....'

'I'll somehow get the money today. Please stop that recital, Ma,' he said.

'You've been saying that for three months now. It's our mistake not to have paid the dowry. No, it's my fault that I bore a son like you. Will you send her back or keep her at home like a widow?'

his mother asked.

Hurt, he hurried outside to head for the canal embankment, with a parting assurance to his mother who continued her tirade.

Outside the hut, Kotesu saw his sister crouching in a corner, a picture of sorrow personified. When she raised her head and looked at him, her big eyes brimmed with tears and contempt at his inability to stop them. 'Maybe, I'm imagining things,' he thought. He was familiar with the contemptuous looks of his mother; perhaps his sister was taking a page from her book.

She knew of his addiction to liquor, of his trips to brothels, but not what he did for a living. He wondered what his mother and sister would do if they knew he robbed corpses. Would they shun him like a leper?

Kotesu reached the locks. At least once a week, some unfortunate person jumped into the Krishna in an attempt at suicide. This week not a single corpse floated downstream. He hoped that at least one would show up and gift five hundred rupees to him.

Kotesu tried to figure out reasons why people killed themselves. Some did it because they were unable to bear the torture inflicted by their husbands, some killed themselves because they scored poor marks in their exams, and some did it for lost loves. Desperate women jumped into the dark waters of the Krishna with no thought for the ornaments on their body. That, of course, suited the likes of Kotesu and Narigadu.

He stopped his philosophizing and screwed up his eyes to look into the water gleaming like a mirror. He'd been keeping a sharp vigil for a couple of hours now. From the changing colours of the water he knew that some object was afloat. Definitely, it had to be a corpse. Corpse of a woman, he hoped. His eyes shone in anticipation. There will be gold on the body if it is a woman, or at least a mangalasutram, he thought.

He needed a mere five hundred. It would bring the light back into his sister's life. She would look at him with love and gratitude in her big shining eyes. He was determined to get her the five hundred rupees even if it meant kissing a rotting corpse.

Five hundred rupees—the price of his sister's happiness! Five hundred to save her marriage, to bring the sunshine back into her life!

The corpse drifted down close to him, wrapped in a dark blue sari, the face sunk in water. The hair was dishevelled and fanned out.

He looked around for a possible competitor. Narigadu was nowhere to be seen. Perhaps he was in police lock-up. He must be groaning in bed after the policeman had given him the works. The thought cheered him up.

The corpse ended its drift at the gates.

'This is mine. I need not struggle with Narigadu like dogs fighting over leftovers. All the gold and the money are mine. Radhabai must get a taste of my manhood for the insults she hurled at me. I'll hurl ten ten-rupee notes at her and make her pick them up like a beggar. That's how I'll avenge my humiliation,' he thought.

Kotesu waded slowly into the water. The water was cold. He got to the corpse and saw a turmeric string around its neck. The mangalasutram must be there too, he thought with glee as he overturned it.

His sister's face shone up at him, so peaceful, her dark eyes finally free of tears, resting behind the closed lids.

THE TRUANT
DADA HAYAT

The ant crawled up his knee and paused to check the terrain with its elbowed antennae. Satisfied there was no possible hazard, it continued to crawl. Chanti's torpid eyes followed the black carpenter ant's journey as it inched forward haltingly. Impulsively, he flicked the insect off with his forefinger. It hit the ground cutting a graceful arc in the air, steadied itself and scuttled away.

The idea of going to school after such an exhilarating engagement with an ant didn't appeal to Chanti. He watched the fleeing ant with his chin resting on his knee. Groping for the pencil stubs and chalk pieces that enjoyed permanent residence in his shorts, he took out a chalk piece. He drew what he intended to be a circle on the black surface of the stoop. He halved the circle with a vertical line, attached two ears and snake-like tresses to its sides, and wrote 'Mother' below. Next to that he drew another form, meant to resemble his father, and crowned it with a clump of hair. He reflected on his creations and, satisfied, proceeded to draw a caricature of his teacher.

His mother came out of the kitchen. She gazed at her son's work of art and smiled admiringly. In a swell of motherly love, she drew him close to her and said, 'Drawing pictures? Don't you have to go to school? Come, brush your teeth and have a shower.'

Chanti had started going to school just two months ago. He'd learnt the alphabet from his mother. He pushed back the locks of tangled hair from his forehead and, pointing to his drawing, said, 'Look, Amma, isn't our teacher pretty?'

'Very nice. Isn't it time for school? Come, get ready,' his mother entreated. He made a face and followed her, unwillingly. After she bathed him and combed his hair, he walked into the kitchen.

Pulling at the hem of her sari, Chanti snuggled up to his mother who was squatting before the stove, in the middle of making a savoury porridge.

'Be still, my child. Let me finish cooking the upma.'

Chanti rested his chin on her shoulder and mustering all his charm cooed, 'Ma....'

'What?'

'Ma...' he repeated, pulling her sari.

'What's the matter?' she asked, slightly irritated.

'Let me skip school today, Ma.'

She stopped her work, stared into his face directly and asked him, 'Why?'

Chanti became sullen, and his mother went back to stirring the upma.

'Ma,' he persisted.

'Ask your father,' she said and dismissed him.

Chanti's face fell and he stood there fussing with the hem of his mother's sari. She freed it from his hands and said, 'Anything else?'

She gently squeezed her son's hand resting on her shoulder and gave in, 'Okay, okay, stay back but make sure you study well at home.'

His face glowing and with plump cheeks puffed out in jubilation, he dashed out of the kitchen and began prowling near his father's room. His father, busy reading a newspaper, turned and looked affectionately at his son.

'What's the matter, child?' he asked.

Chanti clutched the arm of the chair that was barely level with his chin. He said, shyly, 'Pa, Ma wants me to stay at home today.'

'Why?' his father asked, surprised. Tongue tied with fear, Chanti kept looking blankly at him.

Chanti's father shouted into the kitchen, 'Did you tell him to bunk school?'

'Yes,' came the blunt reply from the kitchen.

'Why?'

'He can go tomorrow,' she said.

Confused, his father stepped into the kitchen. Chanti stood still, afraid his father might veto the plan.

His father repeated the question.

'He is tired; he's been playing all of Sunday. I said it's okay because the poor child has never missed any of his classes,' his mother said.

'Doting on him like this is not good for him.'

'Don't make a big fuss. I told you, he'll go tomorrow. It's only been two months that he's been going to school.'

His father strode back to his room, newspaper in hand, without looking at the boy.

Poor Chanti. He stole a glance at his dad's face, sad he'd made him angry. With a heavy heart he clambered on to the stoop. He angrily erased the artwork of the morning, then ran to his sister. She was wrestling with homework on a mat inside the hall. She'd moved inside from her previous station on the veranda, after the morning sun had become unbearable.

He asked her eagerly, 'Sister, shall we play a game of carrom?'

'What, you want me to play with you? I have to finish my homework and go to school!'

Without taking his eyes off the paper their father asked Chanti's sister, 'What were you doing all of yesterday?'

She raised her head and replied indifferently, 'Nothing,' and resumed her schoolwork. Chanti sat cross-legged by her side and tried to read his books while keeping an eye on her activities. After only a few minutes of watching his sister, he was bored. He couldn't make any sense of what she was doing.

He bolted to the sun drenched backyard. The heat rose from the ground. He fixed his eyes on a butterfly perched on a radiant marigold, flapping its multicoloured wings. Chanti tried to trap it in his fist by sneaking up on the flower. But the butterfly flew away and settled on another flower. He tiptoed to the second flower, but it took flight over the compound wall and vanished. Disappointed, he looked around for more butterflies but there were none. 'I should have come out earlier,' he told himself.

He turned his attention to the marigolds but knew that Ma would scold him if he as much as touched them. His eyes travelled to grass flowers at the foot of the wall. He sat down and began plucking them one after the other, his little face puckered in concentration. Suddenly, from the corner of his eye, he saw an earthworm move leisurely through the sun warmed soil. He took a twig and tweaked the worm. It marshalled up some speed and crawled into a burrow hidden behind a clump of grass. He thrust the twig into the burrow to pry it out. No success. He yanked the grass clump. It resisted. Frustrated, he used all his strength to uproot the clump. It came off easily throwing him on his backside into the slush, where his mother had watered the plants earlier. Yuck, he thought.

'Come, eat your upma,' Ma called him from the kitchen. She saw him stomping back to the house through the yard, dejected, with a generous patch of mud on the seat of his pants. She shouted at him, 'Silly boy, I bathed you just a while ago!' Ma gave his cheek a reproachful pinch and dragged him into the bathroom. She took the dirty clothes off, and rapidly washed his feet and hands. His cheek was still smarting and his big eyes filled with angry tears. His mother dressed him in fresh clothes and took him into the kitchen to feed him upma.

Breakfast over, Chanti ran to the front door. He stood there; feet planted firmly apart, hands folded across his chest. The bright street outside was filled with activity. Hari, the boy next door, ran up to him and asked, 'Aren't you coming to school?'

With the pride of a truant, Chanti shook his head importantly.

'Why?'

'Ma asked me not to.'

Confused, the inquisitive Hari demanded a reason. When Chanti told him it was his choice, Hari asked if he was bunking school for good.

'No. I'll return tomorrow,' Chanti said.

'Won't your mother punish you?'

'No,' he said, feeling very special.

He stood there in the doorway for a while after Hari had left. He looked at the busy street outside for a while. Tired, he came inside and busied himself examining the pictures in the Telugu reader. The house was very quiet. His sister had gone to school and father had left for work. He shoved the books aside and came into the hall, already fed up with his day of leisure.

It dawned on Chanti that a weekday was different from Sunday. His sister wasn't around to play ball with. He couldn't climb on to his father's knee and demand to be told a story because he was at work.

The house was empty, echoing with silence.

But Chanti was determined to enjoy this day of playing hooky. He climbed on to his father's armchair and picked a fat tome from the table. He sat dwarfed in the chair, turning pages randomly.

Damn it, no pictures.

He'd asked his father the other day 'What are you reading?'

'It's my book, my child.'

'What's in it?'

'Office things.'

'Oh,' he'd said, pretending to understand what office things meant, and declared knowingly, 'Quite a big book.'

His father had smiled and said, 'You'll read bigger books if you go to school regularly and study well, my boy.'

Images of growing up and reading big books tickled his fancy as he sat in his father's large chair, the big book resting on almost the entire length of his legs. He'd finish his schooling and read all the books his father had read. He took the book from his lap and carefully placed it back on the table. He then ran to his mother, his heart fluttering with the vision of a scholarly future.

'Amma, like father, I'll study all the big books when I'm his age,' he told her solemnly.

'Ah,' she said distantly.

'Such big books,' he said holding out his hands to indicate their size.

'How will you do that, if you don't go to school every day?' His spirits sagged.

She smiled to herself at this sudden change in his mood.

Chanti stole into the backyard. A merciless sun made it impossible to play outside. He walked back into the house and slid again into his father's chair. What would Hari be doing now?

He'd played with him all day yesterday. Hari reminded him of school, and with it came thoughts of the teacher. He loved his teacher. 'She tells such good stories, and never hits me,' he thought.

He remembered the other teacher, the scary one who caked her face in a thick coat of powder, with a red vermilion dot on her forehead. Her outsized spectacles, the loosely braided hair, the cane in her hand, a duster on the table, some chalk pieces, the black board, and all the other teaching paraphernalia strewn everywhere. Though she never beat anyone, she twirled the cane, menacingly. He pictured his desk. It would be empty today, he thought sadly.

He got tired of sitting on the armchair and emerged from his house to check out the street. Some street urchins were playing marbles by the roadside, under a tree. He walked up to them and stood watching the game. He didn't know how to play marbles. One of the players closed his left eye with his left hand and taking aim with the marble in his right hand, shot it deftly at the marble of the rival. Chanti watched this amazing feat of dexterity in awe.

Suddenly, a skirmish erupted. The owner of the vanquished marble shoved the victor with his left hand, accompanied by a verbal volley. The first boy lunged forward and had his rival trapped in the crook of his arm. The second boy jammed his elbow into the first boy's abdomen. Chanti was frightened and fled to the backyard of his house. He wandered around listlessly and collected three small pebbles and began imitating the moves of the marble players. The sun turned hostile and rained down invisible fire. Chanti threw away the pebbles, wondering what to do next.

He approached his mother, who was sifting rice, trying to remove the small granules of dirt and mud.

'Ma, why don't you make a treat for me?'

'I made it just yesterday, my love! How can I make it every day?'

'Ma, please.'

'Your sister is not home today, she'll miss it.'

'That's OK, she can have it some other day.'

'I can't be making sweets every day! I'll make it next Sunday.'

Chanti left the room and wondered why mothers were so unreasonable. He felt really lonely. Seeing as there was nobody to play with, he took out the carrom board and began playing by himself, but was soon fed up with switching places and retrieving the striker that often flew off the board. He left the board on the floor without cleaning up and gathering the coins into their pouch. He peeped out of the front door and found that the marble players had disappeared. He ran to his mother and pestered her for a story.

'Silly boy, I have to finish my chores, I can't just drop everything and tell you a story. Leave me be.'

He moved close to her and tried to rest his head on her lap. She nudged it aside. He remembered his most effective weapon and burst into tears. He fell to the ground and threw a fit, thrashing his feet and bawling. He continued till his mother came and called him.

'Lunch is ready, won't you come and eat it?' she asked gently.

'No, go away.'

'My darling, Chanti, come eat.' She coaxed.

'No.'

'Come, you're my sweetie pie.'

'..........'

'You don't want a sweet treat?'

'A treat?' he cried ecstatically, abruptly rising from the mat where he'd been resting in protest.

'Come, you can have it.'

'No,' Chanti said not relenting.

'Okay, stay there,' she said, tired of his tantrums, and left. He was angry that she'd not tried harder to appease him. But the lure of the candy was too hard to resist; he gave up his stubborn pose and ran after his mother.

An orderly from his father's office came at noon to collect lunch boxes for the master and his schoolgoing children.

'Our little master hasn't gone to school today?' the orderly asked.

'None of your business,' Chanti said belligerently.

'My, my, the little master is angry,' the orderly tried to egg him on.

Chanti sped away to his refuge, the mat, and lay down. His school danced in front of his eyes. He thought of the groups of children playing together during recess, the teacher holding up the Telugu reader in her hand pointing to all the nice pictures and words. Suddenly, a wave of love for his school washed over him, making him regret he'd missed it. He fell asleep thinking of school.

In the evening he stood in front of his house and saw Hari return from school.

'Oye Kiran, you've missed it. The teacher told us a great story today,' said Hari.

'What was the story about?' Chanti asked him eagerly.

'The deer and the jackal.'

'Tell it to me, please,' Chanti pleaded.

'Some other time. The teacher asked for you. She said you've become a spoilt child.'

Chanti's heart sank.

'Kesavam master arranged a kabaddi match with the boys in his class,' said Hari.

'Who won?'

'We did!' Hari said proudly.

Chanti's heart swelled with pride.

After Hari's departure, he played until his father and sister returned home. He ran from one to another in sheer joy, taking turns holding on to each of them.

Before going to bed that night, he asked his mother, 'Ma, what's the story about the deer and the jackal?'

'What deer and what jackal?' Ma asked.

'How do I know? Hari told me.'

'Oh, you mean that,' Ma said and began.

'Once upon a time, a deer lived in the jungle. A jackal tried to befriend the deer so that it could have the deer for lunch later....'

Chanti was all ears. He loved the story. Lost in thoughts about the deer and the jackal, Chanti abruptly raised his head from his mother's shoulder and said, 'Amma, wake me up early tomorrow.'

'Why?' she asked.

'I must go to school,' he said, laying his head back on his mother's shoulder.

AN IDEAL MAN
ADDEPALLI PRABHU

His friend Mahesh had always dreamt of living in an enchanting place that beckoned him like a beautiful girl with windswept hair, wearing hip-hugging jeans. Venkatesh too shared such a fantasy. Today, however, was not the kind of day one would run into such a vision in real life. It began to rain as soon as he had taken off in an auto from Amalapuram. He arrived at his destination, Bodasakurru port, and the rain was still in no mood to relent. On the contrary, it had picked up speed and strength along the way.

He climbed out of the auto and was completely drenched before he could pay the auto driver. He walked down to the launch bay. The mighty Godavari roared angrily before him, helped by the downpour that mercilessly thrashed the earth, in an unrivalled spectacle. The rain continued, noisily. He rushed to the shelter of the awning of a nearby cigarette bunk.

'Is there a launch that will take me to the other side?' he asked the owner of the bunk.

'It is impossible in this rain,' the man said. After a minute he asked, 'Where do you want to go?'

'Adurru,' Venkatesh said.

'Forget it,' the man scoffed.

It was just four in the afternoon but the sky was already dark due to the rain and the clouds. The rain raged, threatening to hold the place hostage for days. Soon, the distinction between the river and the horizon disappeared, uniting the land with the skies. Several boats, small and big, were anchored to their pegs in the bay.

This was no time to panic, Venkatesh thought. He covered his head with his tote and walked into the rain. And not too far away, he found a small hut perched inches above the ground. He was sure to find help, he thought, and sprinted to the hut and peeped inside.

'Hello, hello,' he called.

Inside the hut, a person sitting by a mud stove turned his head and looked at the two feet visible under the door.

'Who's that?' the man shouted above the din of the rain.

Venkatesh replied, 'I need a boat.'

'Please come in, sir, you're soaking,' the man said.

Venkatesh ducked through the low entrance and walked into the hut. A string cot in a corner was in such bad shape that its middle sagged and kissed the ground.

'You're completely drenched, sir, please sit on the cot; I assure you it won't crumble,' the man said.

Venkatesh dropped the bag and hauled himself onto the cot. Water was streaming down his head. Water from inside his boots spilt on the floor and formed a puddle.

'I want a boat to cross the river and someone to ferry me,' he said. His body shuddered from the cold and his teeth chattered when he spoke.

'You're so wet. Please dry your hair with this towel,' the man in the hut said and proffered a piece of cloth.

'No, no, thank you, I have one in my bag,' Venkatesh said and opened his bag. Though the tote was wet, the towel was dry and he sponged his head vigorously with it.

The man stoked the coal fire inside the stove, put a dented aluminium vessel on top and poured water into it.

Seeing Venkatesh still shivering, the hut man retrieved a few embers from the stove, put them in a pan and pushed it under the cot.

'Sir, please keep sitting here, you will get warmer,' the man said and brought two glasses of thick tea. The fragrance of the tea revived the traveller who downed it in two greedy gulps. The tea tasted good despite the jaggery used to sweeten it.

The man then pulled out a bidi from the folds of his lungi and lit it with an ember he picked out from the fire with his bare fingers.

'I must go to Adurru urgently. There is no launch available now. Could you take me in your boat to the other side? I will pay whatever you want,' Venkatesh said.

He had stopped shivering but his soggy clothes clung to him uncomfortably.

The man exhaled a long leisurely breath and asked, 'Where are you from?'

'What business is that of yours?' Venkatesh said, trying to hide his irritation.

The man smiled and said, 'Don't be cross with me, sir. Do you have any idea how heavy the rain is? It's a typhoon. Look, how merciless it is.'

'I don't care if I'm drenched. I must go. Urgently. That's all there is to it,' Venkatesh said.

'No sir, not possible at all.'

'Didn't I say that money is no issue?' Venkatesh said.

'This is not something money can buy, sir. River Godavari is like a goddess possessed. We can do nothing except sit here in safety and witness the river's fury.'

Venkatesh was stunned. The fierce thunder and rain outside were deafening.

'You can go to Amalapuram when the rain relents a bit and take a bus from there to Rajole, get off at Jaggannapet, and take an auto to Adurru,' the man said.

Venkatesh sighed. He'd chosen this route because he wanted to get to Adurru early.

'Are there any lodges around?' he asked.

'Only in Amalapuram, sir. But how will you get there?' the man asked. He got up, lit a lantern, and hung it on a rafter near the roof of the hut. He poked his head out of the hut and shouted,

'Ore Sovudu, Sovudu!'

A seven-year-old boy shot into the hut with a makeshift plastic poncho over his head. He was naked except for a piece of cloth tucked between his legs and around his waist like underwear. His shiny black body merged with the darkness that the lantern couldn't chase away. The boy held a palm reed basket in his hands.

'What heavy rain!' the boy exclaimed. He threw the plastic bag out of the door, hung the basket on the eave, and sat by the fire. A woman entered the hut next, and seeing a stranger sitting on the cot, bolted into the kitchen.

The man took out a towel and began to wipe down the boy. 'Where did you go?' he asked.

The voice of the woman sailed towards them from inside the kitchen. 'Does he ever listen to me? He sloshed through the Godavari. It was so frightening.'

'You stupid brat, did you wade into the river in this rain?' his father asked.

The boy stood up and, pretending to raise an imaginary collar, said, 'What do you think? I am Siranjeevi—what can River Godavari do to me?'

The father laughed and told Venkatesh, 'He is a Chiranjeevi devotee, sir,' referring to the ruling movie star of the moment.

The woman had changed into dry clothes and now began to make noisy preparations for dinner. She set the stove roaring and began to cook the meal. The man raised the lantern's glass shutter and lit another bidi and sat in a corner hugging himself. The boy leapt on his mother's back and started rocking to and fro.

Venkatesh rose from the cot and pushed his bag aside. The embers under the cot had died. He tried to look outside. But where was the outside? It was lost in an impenetrable darkness. The orange light of the lantern travelled out of the hut only to vanish in the shadow of the gloom. The dull patter of the rain persisted. Overhead, coconut fronds danced in response to an occasional breeze.

'The rain may not abate now,' Venkatesh said to the man.

'Yes, when was the last time it rained like this?' the man wondered aloud, staring into the inky void. Venkatesh checked his watch in the light of the lantern. It was not yet seven.

'Where can I go in this rain?' Venkatesh asked.

The man gazed fixedly at the rain, his face bathed in the saffron luminescence of the lantern.

'Where can you go? Nowhere,' he said.

'Then what should I do?' Venkatesh asked irritably.

'Stay here tonight and think of your next step after the rain subsides,' the man said.

The boy came skipping out of the kitchen and vaulted on to the man's back.

'Go put on a shirt. You're running around half naked in this cold,' his father said.

The boy dove inside and returned wearing an outsized shirt and proudly cried, 'Daddy!' The shirt tails brushed his knees and the half sleeves came up to his wrists. In the shadows cast by the lantern and the kitchen fire, the boy looked like an alien from another planet. The boy's father laughed and signalled for the boy to sit on his lap.

Venkatesh was confused and unable to figure out his role in this unfamiliar script. How could he spend the night in this hovel with a family of strangers? But the family, far from feeling uneasy, treated him with all the comfort and ease of an oft-visiting relative. His professional crisis management skills had left him. All he could do now was watch the rain drops unfurl as they descended into the orange orb of the lantern.

Meanwhile, his appetite grew ferocious at the fragrance of fish soup seeping out from the kitchen. He looked at his watch. Half past seven.

'Sovudu,' the boy's mother called from the kitchen. The boy went into the kitchen and returned with a bowl full of steaming rice mixed with fish soup. He sat by his father and began to eat with unabashed relish.

The man's wife brought two plates full of rice and two bowls of fish soup. The man said to Venkatesh, 'Please eat and rest, sir. God will take care of everything in the morning.'

Venkatesh was surprised at his own hunger. He sat down in front of a plate heaped with rice in the shape of a huge pyramid.

'This much rice?' He asked.

'I'm sorry, it is not much, really,' his hostess replied.

'It's hardly anything,' the man said.

'No, no. Please remove some,' Venkatesh said.

She brought a big dish containing fragrant, steaming, white rice from the kitchen and took back some from his plate into the vessel.

He mixed the rice with soup and even before he could transfer some to his mouth, there was a flood of saliva and he began drooling. He couldn't remember losing control like this since he was very little. He accepted several more helpings and wondered if he had ever experienced such indescribable joy.

After dinner, he checked the time again and took out his mobile. There was no signal. There was nothing he could do now except to lie down and go to sleep.

The boy dozed off almost immediately after he'd finished his meal. His mother carried him inside and went to bed.

The man cleared the dishes, lit a bidi, and sat down. Venkatesh was embarrassed that he had been drawn into an awkward situation and left with no choice. Surprisingly, his host too seemed to share his feelings.

Venkatesh took out a pair of shorts from his bag, and changed out of his wet clothes behind the cover of his towel. He pulled on a fresh shirt and hung out the wet clothes to dry on a palm rafter.

His head buzzed with thoughts: look at this small hut, their near-naked boy, a shack without electricity, without TV, a dining table or sofa or refrigerator. What kind of a life did these people lead? No goals, no ambition, no killer instinct to climb the social ladder. Like animals, they eat to live and live to eat. Is that all there was to their life? Had they ever heard of Einstein, or Newton, George Bush, Bill Gates, or at least Satyam Computers? Ignorance and poverty!

Meanwhile, the man went inside and brought out a fraying mat and a quilt of unknown vintage. He placed them beside the cot and said to Venkatesh, 'Please sleep. We'll worry about the rest in the morning.' He spread a jute mat for himself on the floor and lay down on it.

The lantern's dim light shone warmly on Venkatesh like a friend. He unrolled the mat and moved it to a dry patch on the floor and decided to do without the quilt. There was a bed sheet in his bag which he retrieved and spread on the mat. He used his rolled-up towel as a pillow.

The darkness outside was total. He checked the time on his mobile and chuckled—he'd never gone to bed this early.

When he opened his eyes it was light outside. But there was no change in the mood of the rain or in the force of the intimidating wind.

The boy was perched like a bird where his father had sat the night before, peering out.

'Where are your parents?' asked Venkatesh. The boy held up two fingers, the universal sign for going to the bathroom.

Venkatesh got up and looked out through the doorway. The river was lapping at its bank. The other bank was invisible. The river seemed to flow directly into the sky. He stretched out his hand and his heart skipped a beat. The rain was fierce and piercing, and came down in sheets, cutting off visibility beyond a few feet. Curtains of water shrouded everything including the vegetation. From behind the watery cascade emerged his host, covered in a plastic sheet from head to toe.

'It's not going to stop now, not for a while. Mad, mad rain. The orchard by the ridge and the harbour have gone under water. Look at the river. If it rises anymore, we'll have to abandon the hut and flee. If you want to leave, cover yourself with this bag and take that route,' the man said, and shivering, he pointed the way to the visitor.

'Where's your mother?' he asked his son.

With the bag on his head Venkatesh stepped into the knee-deep water. He sloshed through the muddy water for a short distance and came back, partly drenched. His feet were encased in mud. He saw the man sitting on the floor of the hut with his wife and son. When she saw Venkatesh coming back, she moved the child into her lap to make place for him. Venkatesh spread the mat he'd slept on earlier and sat down.

'Make some tea, woman', the man ordered his wife.

She hugged the boy close and, sneaking a look at Venkatesh from the corner of her eye, said, 'But there is no jaggery.'

'Make it without jaggery, then!'

'But I can't kindle the stove in this wet weather. Do it yourself,' she said.

The man went to the kitchen and after persistently blowing at the wet fuel managed to start a fire. The boy abandoned the mother's lap and rushed to sit by his father near the fire.

A few minutes later, the man brought two tall glasses filled with boiling black water and passed one to Venkatesh. He sipped it cautiously. At first it had no taste, as though it was just hot water, but as he continued to drink there were hints of an agreeable bittersweet taste.

He asked, 'What's your son's name?'

'Somaraju. I gave him my father's name.'

'The boy looks sharp. Does he go to school?'

'What school?' he scoffed. 'Idling time away in a school won't feed us.'

Thinking that he meant that only idle guys went to school, Venkatesh said, 'No, no. You can get a good job if you study. The boy will earn a lot and prosper.'

'You're right. But how can he make a living without learning to fish?'

Venkatesh was amused. The man had no clue what a job was. That's why these people never get ahead in life, he thought.

'No, my dear man. Education teaches you many things. You can become famous. There is a boy I know, a slip of a brat. Ask him the names of countries anywhere in the world and the presidents of these countries…he'll tell you the correct answers in a snap. He was on TV too. It's all because of education,' Venkatesh said.

The man threw the bidi away and said, 'True, sir. My boy is very sharp too. He can tell you everything about the fish in the Godavari and the sea. Ask him, he'll tell you all the types of fish that swim in the waters. Nobody in the entire neighbourhood knows the names of so many fish. Ore, Sovudu, tell this sir the names of the fish we catch,' he asked his son.

The boy looked at his dad and the visitor and rattled off, 'Catla catla, lobeo rohita, air-breathing fish, channa punctatus, mystus singhala, hill stream fish, garra kempi, ornamental fish, anchovy, giant moray, pacific sergeant, sea goldie….'

Initially, Venkatesh felt annoyed at this fish nonsense. However, soon the condescending smile on his face disappeared.

True, the boy did know all there was to know about fish. He could swim the Godavari in spate, even in the dark. His own son could recite the names of twenty countries and their presidents. It was possible only because it was all study and no play for him from the time he was five years old. But what use were these facts to his son at his age? The teachers were just cramming useless information into their little brains in the name of 'general knowledge'. Who was better off, his son or this boy who understood every nuance of his environment? Wasn't this education? Wasn't this 'knowledge'?

Venkatesh was beset with doubts. 'This boy Sovudu will never earn much,' he told himself, 'neither money nor fame. All his knowledge about rivers, the sea, and fish will perish in the market. Some good-for-nothing fellow will study marine biology and technology spending lakhs of rupees, scour the seas on a computer, and earn millions. This boy, with all his knowledge and skill, will be dredging some muddy pond for fish.' Comforted by such thoughts, Venkatesh fell into a deep sleep.

He woke up to the smell of cooking. He looked out of the hut and saw that it had stopped raining—only a few halting drops fell now and then.

'I think I can leave now,' he said to the man.

'Yes sir, you can reach Amalapuram if you leave early,' said the man and nodded.

'Cook some rice for our visitor,' he told his wife.

Venkatesh was hungry but said, 'Please don't bother. I'm going to Amalapuram anyway.' He squeezed his bed linen and wet clothes into the tote bag and was all set in his shorts and shirt.

The woman brought a bowl of rice and soup and placed it near the cot. The visitor ate it greedily in his haste and, once done, pulled on his shoes over his bare feet and flung the bag over his shoulder, ready to leave. He looked around to make sure he hadn't left anything behind.

The woman and the boy holding her sari stood at the doorway to see him off. The man got ready to accompany him. Involuntarily, Venkatesh pressed his palms together in gratitude. He said to his hostess, 'You've treated me with more affection than my own sister. Thank you.'

Her dark face reddened with embarrassment. She averted her gaze and drew the boy closer to her.

'We can't go that way. The harbour is under water.' The man said to Venkatesh as soon as they came out of the hut.

Venkatesh looked in the direction of the harbour and saw only the tip of the ridge. Godavari was dizzying and scary, eddying furiously like a mythical force. It was beautiful and frightening at once.

The man was wading through knee-deep water in front of the

hut. Venkatesh took every step cautiously. The force of the rain had abated but a thin drizzle fell obstinately. Half an hour later they came upon a narrow strip of road. The man stopped and told the visitor, 'This is your route. Go straight; you'll see the centre there.' He narrowed his eyes and saw an auto coming towards them.

'Come, let us ask him if he'll take you.'

The auto stopped. The man went to him and returned quickly, 'The auto has a problem.'

Venkatesh stood there soaking in the rain. The man said, 'If we walk further we'll reach Peruru agraharam. From there you could take an auto and reach Amalapuram. If the roads are kind to you, you can go to Adurru from there.'

'How?' asked Venkatesh.

The man laughed and said, 'You can walk.'

Venkatesh was surprised—how could he have forgotten that he had two feet to walk with?

'Okay, sir. I'll take leave. If the Godavari rises any further, our hut will disappear,' said the man.

'You're right,' said Venkatesh and pulled out a purse from his bag and took out two hundred-rupee notes from it.

'Please keep this,' he told the man and held out the money to him.

'No, sir, that's not right,' the man said dropping his bidi on the road.

'It's alright. I shudder at the thought of what would have happened to me if you hadn't taken me in. You looked after me as if I were your own flesh and blood. That's why it's alright,' said Venkatesh.

The man laughed. He said, 'Sir, it's alright and fair to make money when the other person is in a position to bargain. It is not proper to exploit a person in distress. You are a human being. I'm one too. The tree shelters all birds from the rain. Same principle applies here too.'

Venkatesh put the money back in his wallet and adjusted the

bag over his shoulder.

The man continued, 'If we don't help one another how can we call ourselves human beings? If I were to stand outside your door, stranded, would you let me in or throw me out? Anyway, sir. Please get going; I have to go now. Goodbye,' he bowed and turned around to retrace his path home.

Venkatesh stood staring in the direction of the receding figure. He was afraid to consider his answer to the man's question because he knew it would shame him.

ADIEU, BA

BAA RAHAMATHULLA

Relatives who had come for the last rites and other Muslims from our village pressed around our father Ba's body. A great friend of his, Neelisetti Venkateswarlu, had just arrived to pay his last respects. I told him, 'We've already covered his face and wrapped him in the shroud a while ago. You will have to wait and see him at the masjid.'

Amidst the wailing of women, and the men chanting 'Allahu Akbar', we lifted the coffin on to our shoulders. My elder brother and I were at the head of the bier, my younger brother and my son carried the rear. We wended our way out of the house.

Shifting it from shoulder to shoulder, we carried the coffin into the masjid. At the masjid, my brother-in-law chanted the funeral prayer.

A relative uncovered Ba's face and called out, 'Those who haven't seen Ba may approach and take a quick look.' Neelisetti hurried down the masjid steps and went to the coffin, teary-eyed and sobbing softly.

'Look at the tears in the eyes of the merchant, a high caste man, a wealthy man! Yet he walked all the way to the masjid for a last look at Jungli,' said a young man.

There is a story behind why Ba was called Jungli. When Grandma Agamma had complained of labour pains, her kin took her to the Ongole hospital in a cart. But on the way at Pernamitta the pains became acute. They stopped the cart and lay Grandma on a green patch behind a jungle-like growth at the foot of the hillock. There she delivered Ba. The name Jungli stuck to him because he was born in the woods. His original name was Sheik Abdul Gaffoor, a name even I wasn't aware of for a long time. If someone asked my siblings or me who our father was, we would say, 'We are the sons of Jungli.'

It wasn't just Ba, all his cart-driver friends had similar monikers: Kya Faida (Useless), Galaata (Ruckus), Budda (Old Guy), Chowtodu (Deaf One), Paatifilm, Tapaal, Angaal Kaadi, Hattu Budda, Budda Mowli, etc. They used to visit our house frequently when we were kids. Yet, I don't know their real names even now. I doubt that even they know their own names or dates of birth. We can't blame them. Our forebears didn't know how to read or write. Take any Muslim family in our village—none of them have ever gone to school.

That's why mother had urged Ba every day since their marriage, 'See even the children of Malas and Madigas are going to school. It is only the Muslim children who stay at home. We should send our children to school too.'

Such words had always hurt Ba like the wound on our bull's neck. 'Stupid woman, this has become a daily ritual for you. Am I not pouring into your hands all that I earn every day? Do whatever you want with it: pass the thread through the eye of the needle or buy slate pencils,' Ba would say and light a bidi.

Truth be told, if Ma had not pestered Ba I wouldn't have this job or the comfortable life I lead now. Like all the children of all the other Saibus—the Muslims—I'd be pulling a cart or pedalling a sewing machine. That's why Ma used to say, 'If I'd kept quiet, you would have, like your Ba, been prodding the ass of a bull all your life.'

The last journey started. We reached the grave dug for Ba, reciting the Kalama Ashahadun, 'la ilaha illallaaha mohamadan rasoolillah', 'there is only one God, and that God is Allah', and gently lowered his body into it. He looked as if in deep sleep. After the Imam of the masjid blessed his soul, each one of us sprinkled earth on the body, placed a jujube branch at his head, lit joss sticks around him, and headed back home.

On the way, Ba's memories filled my mind.

⌒

The morning had always begun early for Ba. The very first thing he did was ready the cart and untie the bull tethered to the dibble. He would then lift the shaft of the cart and the bull would get under the yoke quietly. After harnessing it, he'd caress the animal's hump and pat it. The bull then knew it was time to start the day.

We belong to Santhanuthalapadu, which is neither a village nor a town. It is surrounded by more such nondescript villages. Most of the Saibus in our village made a living by renting carts. Our cart travelled mostly to Gudipadu, Gummanampadu, Madduluru, Bandlamudi, and several other villages. For a while, the cart picked up people whose destination was Chimakurthy or Ongole. A few times, it even transported corpses in the secrecy of the night; a lot of courage was needed to accept such cargo. During the tobacco-planting season, Ba would ferry stacks of tobacco saplings. He also accepted passengers going to carnivals at Jallapalem, Gummanampadu, Ramateertham, and Kuntiganga.

There are only a couple of Brahmin families in our village. Subbayya's family went out to neighbouring villages to perform priestly ceremonies and brought back rice, lentils, and other food items gifted to them in return for their services. It was the job of our Dada, our grandfather, and Ba to bring them back. There were four or five such trips in a month and the monthly fare only amounted to two and a half annas. The Brahmins would sometimes share their takings with Ba.

Ba was never choosy about picking up passengers. Sometimes, there wouldn't be any passengers or cargo to carry. After he got the Guravareddy Palem contract, he never travelled to other places and the cart returned to the bazaar before it was dark. He collected goods from the shops of Grendols, Maddols, and Neelisettis. He lifted the goods himself, bags of rice, oil tins, and large sacks of other items. He would carry a hundred-kilo rice bag on his back and hoist it onto the rear of the cart with ease. Lest the shaft go up, he would ask me to sit on it. This loading business went on for an hour; I'd be sitting there throughout. Oblivious to the world outside, Ba went through his work like a machine, with the concentration of a saint lost in meditation, sweat streaming down his body and soaking the ground.

He'd drive the fully loaded cart and always stop it at the mouth of our lane. 'Boy, mind the cart,' he'd tell me and go inside the house. I kept a watch over the cart until he finished his meal and came out with a tiffin carrier stuffed with food. His breakfast consisted of rice mixed with fermented gruel. I'd watch the bull and the heavy load it carried and feel its pain, as if I were the one carrying that weight. I would shoo away crows and kites trying to perch on the bull. When I saw Ba, I'd drive the cart to the fresh water well. The bull would surge forward if I twisted its tail and cried 'hai, hai'. If I yanked the rein and swung it to the left over the hump, the bull would turn left. I'd yank the reins to the right and the bull would turn right. If I tugged at the rein, the bull would stop as if on cue. I enjoyed driving the cart. Ba would say, 'Oy, go to school and get a job. You can sit under a fan and work. The cart man's life is misery—eat when there is work and starve when there isn't.' When I'd jump off the cart, Ba would press a small coin into my palm and say, 'jatan ja, go carefully', and drive away in the cart, leaving me behind.

Shopkeepers at Guravareddy Palem and other important townspeople would ask Ba to bring goods for them. The merchants of Santhanuthalapadu were his friends and he'd negotiate loans for them. They all thought him a trustworthy and peace-loving man. He served the village for a long time in this way. His friends used to say, 'This Jungli ate away all the money of Guravareddy Palem and in turn Guravareddy Palem ate away all his money.' He'd carry bundles of notes for them, squeezing them into the folds of his lungi.

On the way, Ba would commit to memory, and repeat for hours, the names of the recipients and the sums owed to them.

One day, I accompanied Ba, sitting on the bags in the cart like an emperor. After we crossed the village limits, the fragrance of the grass and a cool breeze elated me. The cart was proceeding on a tar road flanked on one side by paddy fields and a ridge on the other. Ba looked up and felt the sun was still low in the sky and hoped to reach Guravareddy Palem before the sun turned unkind because the damned bull would gasp if the weather grew hot. Together, the rice bags and the oil tins must have weighed six to seven quintals. He lit a bidi. Smoking contentedly, he reminded himself what cargo he'd picked up from whom, the names of the persons who were to receive it, and the monies to be collected from each. That recounting took the weight off his chest.

The cart now passed the well of the Sallas and got on to the dirt road to Mynampadu. This road is full of potholes until Rudravaram, so he had to drive with care. Sometimes, he would get down and push the cart, manually propelling the spokes, shouting loudly at the bull. Any carelessness would result in a broken axle or the wheels getting stuck in a furrow and the bull would buckle and drop down onto its forefeet. To hoist it back onto its feet was no easy job. We struggled to get to Challapalem, a small village on the way. It only got worse from there. There was no track of any kind from Challapalem to Guravareddy Palem. We had to take shortcuts across fields. To get the cart over the bumps was tough. You had to press the shaft down with one hand and move the wheel with the other. Any loss of balance or grip would result in a crash. There was nobody nearby to help. Managing one bump after another was near-fatal. For that reason alone, it was impossible for anyone to redeem their debt to Ba and his animal.

The sun was just getting down to business when we reached Guravareddy Palem. After unloading the cargo at various addresses, he stationed the cart under the neem tree in the village centre and anchored the animal to the wheel. He borrowed a bucket from Anasuyamma's house and bought half a kilo of jaggery at Setti's shop. He drew water from a well, mixed the jaggery in it, and fed the slush to the bull. He placed a bundle of hay from the underside of the cart in front of the bull for it to graze on. We then set out to collect dues from the traders.

When the sun was right over our heads, we opened our aluminium lunch carrier, and under the neem tree, ate a meal of rice, a chutney of cucumber seeds, and broiled dry fish. Ba bought for me a plate of rice fritters from Pevamma's hole-in-the-wall eatery. When we were done, we yoked the bull once more and briefly stopped the cart in front of a tea bunk. He swigged a cup of tea and bought a pack of bidis. He also got some candy for me, and two bananas that he thrust into the bull's mouth.

'Saibu, you're the only man I've ever seen who buys bananas with his hard-earned money only to feed them to his animal. You seem to be a crazy fellow,' said the man in the shop as he accepted the money.

'This poor voiceless animal pulls my cart, earns money for me, and feeds my family. If I don't feed it well, it is as good as eating its shit,' Ba retorted.

Ba lived life on its terms—he knew how to be happy with what life offered him. He rarely spent any time thinking nor did he pray at the masjid. He could only manage to visit the idgah on the occasion of Bakrid and during Ramzan. Ba's memories left a hole in my heart.

My grandfather also plied a bullock cart. Ba would lurk in wait when Dada's cart was all set to leave for the day's rounds. He'd skip school, crouch behind the cart, and follow it unseen. When the cart reached the outskirts of the village someone would spot Ba and tell Dada about it. Left with no alternative, Dada would let him onto the cart. That's how the bullock cart entered Ba's life. Poor people have no place in their lives for school or reflection. There was no question of Ba learning anything at all.

'Give me ten rupees. I want a Thums Up soda,' my son broke my reverie. I was also thirsty but in no mood for a drink. I gave him the money and returned to my past.

In the beginning Dada would negotiate the fare and Ba would make the trip for the clients. Dada would collect the fare later. After a while Ba began collecting the fare and handing it to Dadi, my grandmother. After Ba got married, he'd give the day's takings to Ma.

Ba never kept money with him. The bull would do its job and rest when there was no errand. In the same way, Ba also rested and looked at the ceiling when he wasn't driving the cart.

Whenever I asked him if he needed money, he'd say, 'What will I do with it?' I haven't met any other person who didn't know what to do with money.

My Dada spent all his life driving the cart. For decades, the cart had been a part of our family. There was food at home only when the cart was engaged. In the Saibu neighbourhood, at least ten Saibus owned carts. As a matter of fact, most cart men were Saibus. The Gollas, Vadderas, and Mala castes sold grass. Our supplier of grass was Mala Subbi. Every evening, she delivered a stack of grass to us. It had a magical smell that spread to the entire house when she opened the bundle. As soon as the stack was placed before it, the bull would rush and shove its mouth into the grass. I searched the grass for chana beans and red gram pods; Subbi hid them in the grass for me to find. In contrast to others who fed one bundle of grass to their animals, Ba would feed our bull two. Half of Ba's earnings went to buy sesame and coconut waste, black and brown jaggery, bran, and grass for the animal. The balance went to the Vaddes for making the axle, the wheels, and for shoeing the bull, to the Medaras for making the hood, and to the Madigas for making the whips.

Want in our family is a legacy as old as our grandfather, Dada. When he was little, Ba ate black cotton soil mixed with curd when there was no food at home. My Dada would walk twenty miles to Podili for a day's labour but Ba rarely left our village. Long ago, he'd gone to Sholapur to bring home a horse. For cattle, he would go south. It took two to three days for him to buy them at Velupodu near Dagadarthi and come home through Kavali, breaking the journey there. When he was in one of his good moods, he would boast about two things to his friends: 'My marriage went on not for a day or two but for a whole week. We brought a dancing horse from the south. How grand do you think it was? Like a camel. We plied it with liquor and made it dance for two nights.' His eyes would go up and touch his brow after he finished narrating. When revealing the second thing, he would puff out his already swollen chest. 'No Saibu, cart Saibu, tailor Saibu, or any other Saibu in the entire neighbourhood, sent his children to school. Except this Jungli. Not some apology of a school. My son finished his B. A. and got a proper job afterwards.'

Ba would often bring home treats for us—red gram beans, young tamarind fruit, and fig fruit, all plucked from the fields on the way home. My favourite was when Ba would bring chana plants with lots of pods. He'd throw them into burning hay that was always in plenty at home. He'd retrieve them from the fire before they were fully burnt and wake us up, ignoring Ma's pleas. We sat around the fire warming ourselves and ate the snack. He enjoyed the sight of us eating, and looked at us with adoration. He gave us jaggery to eat with it too. The young green chana roasted in a hay fire is very tasty. In the millet season, he'd get Grandma to make millet candy. She made the candy at night, lest we eat all of it before it was ready. Ba would pinch our buttocks to wake us up. Seduced by the fragrance of the candy we'd get up, sit around the deep fryer, and eat. Sometimes he'd buy a sick goat, take it to a butcher and bring home its meat. Ba was quite fond of fish and meat.

My son, who'd been listening to my stories of Ba, went to bed saying he wanted to sleep. I closed my eyes trying to sleep but the welter of thoughts coursing through my mind wouldn't let me.

Like the collapse of the Babri Masjid, the axle of our cart collapsed one year. With the number of red buses to Guravareddy Palem increasing, people preferred buses to carry their cargo. They dispensed with the services of cart drivers. Ba didn't care to replace the axle. His cart career, which began with the dawn of Independence, ended in this manner.

Ba's friends also said goodbye to plying carts. Scorched in the sun and soaked in rain, our cart slowly came apart. Ma consigned its parts, one by one, to the fire to cook food for us. The epilogue came when Ba sold the animal to meet the bill for a caesarean surgery for one of my sisters.

For us Saibus, plying horse-drawn carriages and bullock carts, tailoring, and ginning were trades for generations. Now they have lost their usefulness to society. Ba switched to a handcart that he pulled for ten years taking oil tins and sundry goods from one shop to another. In his last days, Ba's life resembled the life of the bull he'd sold. He hadn't heard of computers, hi-tech products, or Pakistan, Ayodhya, or Gujarat, though all of them happened in his lifetime.

∽

'We'd never imagined he'd leave us so soon. He'd complained of chest pain and gone to rest on his handcart. That's all,' my brother told someone who came to commiserate. Ma cried endlessly. I didn't. My mind was a vacuum—a good cry would have brought some relief from the grief.

On the third day of the last rites, we brothers and a group of men from the masjid went to Ba's tomb. The men from the masjid blessed us after we'd placed puffed rice, chana dal, and coconut pieces mixed with jaggery at the tomb. They said, 'The tomb is the permanent home for a Muslim. Wash it well and go home,' and took their leave. We, the three brothers, stayed back. We mixed mud and water and made a small shrine from the mixture. On the way home we remembered that Ba couldn't do without a bidi even for an hour. We returned to the tomb with a pack of Bavuta bidis and a matchbox and placed them on Ba's tomb.

After the tenth day, we took leave of Ma promising to come back for the fortieth day services when the deceased cuts the last ties to their past life. At the bus stand, we were reminded of Ba's customary warm welcomes and farewells. Whenever we, his children, visited the village, Ba, who stood waiting on the porch, would greet us by walking down towards us. He'd collect our luggage from us. He'd repeat the same sequence when we took his leave. He'd see us off till we disappeared from his sight. A man of such abundant love knows no death.

> In the tomb of our hearts
> Ba's love is like an ocean.

MORNING STAR

PALAGIRI VISWAPRASAD

The village was in mourning. A murder had been committed three days earlier. The panchayat president, his sons, and their henchmen were all on the run.

Sujatha sat in the veranda, disoriented, leaning against a pillar. Women clustered around her, close relatives of the victim. Ravindra Reddi's mother lay on a string cot, semi-conscious. Two of his brothers were busy overseeing plans for the funeral.

Sujatha had been marshalling all the strength in her body to cope with her husband's death. With every commiserating visitor, her wounds bled afresh, and she couldn't stop crying. Thoughts of a lonely life assaulted her like an unsolicited menace.

The village had been free of tension since the murder of the panchayat president's younger son a few months earlier. Ravindra Reddi, his brothers, and three others stood trial for that murder. The High Court threw out the case. The village had limped back to its even keel.

By nature, Ravindra Reddi had not been the vengeful sort. He had not let anyone in his group go after the other side for implicating them. The enemy too did nothing to disturb the uneasy calm. The assembly and municipal polls had also been conducted peacefully. The killing of Ravindra Reddi thus came as a complete shock to everyone.

On that fateful day, Ravindra Reddi rose with the sun, ate leftover rice for breakfast, and left for Proddatur with two farmhands. Half an hour later the whole village was agog: unidentified assailants had tossed bombs at him at Durgamma Vanka.

The life had drained out of Sujatha when she heard the news. She had boarded her brother-in-law's tractor in a daze and headed towards the spot. They had passed a steady stream of villagers heading in the same direction as if on a pilgrimage. By the time they got to Durgamma Vanka, a big crowd had already gathered from the surrounding hamlets. The MLA's brother had arrived as well. Sujatha had prayed desperately for her husband's life on the way to the scene, hoping that the bomb was not that deadly.

The crowd had parted for the family. Ravindra Reddi's body lay sprawled face down in the vanka, a small stream. The muddy earth had been soaked in his blood.

Sujatha had fallen to the ground, unconscious. The MLA's brother had arranged for the post-mortem and bribed the authorities for the quick release of the body, a bundle of finely dissected flesh, with the head intact.

The MLA had postponed his political wheeling and dealing in the capital and headed to the village to attend the funeral and pay his respects to Ravindra Reddi's family. Seasoned politicians like him understand the importance of calming tempers and keeping the peace among their constituents.

The village was overrun with local elders and leaders from the MLA's party who had come to mark their presence at the cremation. The crowds dispersed soon after the funeral and Sujatha was left to put her life back together, along with those of her five-year-old daughter and seven-year-old son.

She was not a stranger to political retribution, though she and her father were firmly opposed to it. Her aunt, Saradamma, had been widowed four years into her marriage when her husband was ambushed and hacked to death with sickles by rivals. Devastated at his sister's fate, Sujatha's father had made sure that his two older daughters were married into non-political families, one to a businessman and the other to a government official. Whenever his wife complained that they were too far way and she couldn't meet her grandchildren as often as she would like, he would tell her to be thankful that her sons-in-law were still alive.

Ravindra Reddi's match came highly recommended. Sujatha's father had been very reluctant, but the boy's father said that his son was not interested in politics and was completing his M. Sc. to pursue a career outside the village. Her father finally relented. She had no say in the matter; she married Ravindra Reddi. Though the family was heavily involved in politics, they had a special affection for Ravindra Reddi and his educated wife, an affection that Sujatha occasionally found suffocatingly intense.

A year passed by and Ravindra was yet to find a job. His father had narrowly lost an election a month earlier. As Ravindra's father was heading to the fields with his assistant, his political rival, who had won the election by seven votes, had him killed. His father must have lowered his guard thinking that his defeat would not invite vengeance, but the narrowness of the victory had been motive enough. The rival's men pounced upon Ravindra Reddi's father with scythes. His assistant Jayudu tried to help him, but the thugs pushed him aside and, chasing the victim through the fields, beheaded him. The recently elected panchayat president and his aides were implicated in the case.

It was then that Ravindra Reddi relegated his job search to the backburner and started to make the rounds of the court to prosecute the case. Another three years passed while Ravindra Reddi stayed busy with the case, with the farm, and with party affairs. He lost the case. His mother and brother dissuaded him from lodging an appeal at a higher court. It wasn't until a month later he found out why.

His brother and his friends had stabbed the president's younger son. Ravindra Reddi was cited as the principal accused in that case. With the help of the MLA, he tried, unsuccessfully, to have his name dropped from the case.

Ravindra Reddi now began a merry-go-round of visits to the

courts, the police station, and the bail office, all of which crushed Sujatha's spirit. His mother remained unaffected and, secretly, felt proud that her sons had avenged the death of her husband.

When Ravindra Reddi at last made bail, Sujatha urged him to leave the village and move to the town. 'We can sell our land and possessions and start a business,' she pleaded. Her parents too tried to prevail upon him. Ravindra Reddi turned a deaf ear. The trial went on for four more years, after which the district court sentenced Ravindra Reddi and two others to life in prison. His brothers and the rest of the accused were acquitted. His transfer to the central jail in Rajahmundry dashed all of Sujatha's hopes of his release.

Eighteen months later, the high court ruled in his favour, and Ravindra returned home. He cautioned his supporters not to start the killings afresh. The rivals too were quiet, and peace returned to the village.

Sujatha had revived her pleas to her husband to move to the town. But Ravindra Reddi was not one to turn away from his family or political party. He had his brothers to take care of, the farm to run, and the complex affairs of the party needed his constant attention. Her fear that their children's lives were in danger was met with amusement and impatience. His reputation and social standing were at stake. Bickering, followed by long silences, became a daily routine for them.

Ravindra Reddi's life started following the trajectory of his father's. He strengthened his ties with the MLA, arranging political deals, accepting contracts. He ran the farm in his spare time. Sujatha resigned herself to a life of helpless anxiety.

But even that life was not meant to be, now that Ravindra Reddi was dead. The final ceremonies were placed on hold until the court ruled on his murder. This was the custom in this land where political killings were more common than natural deaths. As the days passed, Sujatha began to surface from her grief, with frequent visits from her parents. Her brothers-in-law assured her, 'We will avenge the death of our brother, you wait and see.'

She did not crave revenge. There were many women who wouldn't rest until their husbands were avenged. Her mother-in-law was a prime example. She had incited her younger sons to avenge their father's death. Her aunt Saradamma was another. When she couldn't persuade her brothers-in-law, it was rumoured that she started an affair with a farmhand to get his cooperation. In fact, when Sujatha was very young, she had once seen the farmhand Ramudu put his hand on her aunt's shoulder, a gesture of unthinkable familiarity considering their different standings in the social hierarchy. When she reported this incident to her mother, she was warned to keep her mouth shut if she didn't want to get thrashed by her father. Shortly after that, Saradamma's younger brother-in-law and Ramudu assassinated the leader of the other party while he was making merry with a woman named Rangi. Both Ramudu and Rangi disappeared the next day. Rumours linking Saradamma and Ramudu and Rangi circulated for a while.

Sujatha had felt repulsed by her aunt's sordid saga. But there was an element of passionate courage, where the love of her husband meant more to her than her own honour and reputation. Sujatha now wondered if her aunt and mother-in-law were perhaps right, and were actually more devoted to their husbands than she had been to hers.

Finally, she made a decision. It was a cold evening towards the end of the waning lunar fortnight of December. As the household was preparing for bed, she announced that she wanted to talk to them. They were surprised but none of them protested, such was the respect they had for her. She took a deep breath and launched into her long monologue.

The family listened in silence.

'Is this why you asked me to come here?' asked her father, surprised.

'Yes,' said Sujatha.

'Have we ever denied you anything? Why do you demand your share of the property? Why do you want to leave the village with the children?' asked her mother-in-law.

'You have never denied me the smallest comfort. I do not want my young brother-in-law and my son to end up like my father-in-law and husband. Let us all leave the village and find a safer place to live,' said Sujatha firmly.

'Why are you so scared?' her mother-in-law asked.

'It's not the fear of death. But this is no way to live. An endless cycle of killings and retribution. You chose to send your children into this battle. I will not do that to mine.'

'Death will come wherever you are. We cannot escape it,' her mother-in-law retorted.

'What a strange philosophy! Any kind of death is better than the one that was meted out to your husband and mine. I do not want my children to be sucked into this cesspool of fear, vengeance, and wickedness,' sobbed Sujatha.

Sujatha's father stepped in and said, 'Let's go home. Why should it be said that the daughter-in-law walked out with her share of property while her husband's body was still warm?'

Sujatha was stung by the innuendo. 'I do not care about the property. I want my children to get a good education, have a safe and decent life. I want to keep them away from these incubators of hate and vengeance. I can take care of myself and my children. My decision will not change,' she said.

There was an uncomfortable silence. The two brothers-in-law excused themselves on some pretext, without any recrimination or rancour. Sujatha's sister-in-law said quietly, 'You have finally said what needed to be said for all these years. No matter how rich we are, our lives will remain mired in this filth. It is better to leave instead of clinging to this land and wallowing in dirty party politics.'

Sujatha's mother-in-law looked daggers at her and muttered to herself, 'This madness seems to be infectious. Everyone wants to leave this house.' She announced loudly, 'Do as you wish. I have one foot in the grave. What do I care? Anyway, times have changed. It is a shame that people today will dishonour their dead by letting their killings go unavenged.'

With great difficulty, Sujatha held her tongue in deference to her father who was standing by her, looking uncomfortable. The old woman delivered another taunt and left.

Sujatha went up to the terrace with her children to sleep. The sky was packed with blinking stars. Conflicting emotions set her heart pounding. Happiness at the prospect of getting away from the village just like she had always dreamed, anxiety that she was stepping into unknown territory. Would her departure douse the fires of revenge? Was it really possible to destroy an ancient malady with such deep roots? But she took comfort in the knowledge that her decision was not a selfish one, but an effort to end the strife within the family.

The starlit night became chilly. She pulled a thick blanket over her kids and herself and surrendered to sleep at last.

A star appeared in the east and shone brightly.

EYE-OPENER
CHADUVULA BABU

It is eleven o'clock at night. My son and his wife are watching a serial on the TV. Waiting for them to turn it off, I keep walking round and round in the front yard. The stereophonic sound of the TV torments me even when I'm outside and unsettles my peace.

A Hero Honda motorbike stops in front of the house across the road. Without alighting, the rider blares the horn as if it were a wake-up call for the entire neighbourhood. He is probably around thirty years old. I wander into his view but fail to get a nod of recognition or even a miserly smile from him. He turns his head away just when our eyes are about to meet. He is wearing a buttoned-up white striped shirt with rolled up sleeves over a pair of black trousers. His hair is in organized disarray. There is an air of great unconcern and lack of urgency about him. I'm familiar with such people.

The boy's mother comes out wearily and opens the gate. The vehicle zooms into the compound, which is devoid of any vegetation. As a regular watcher, I have come to understand that this is the time he gets home every night. In the mornings, I am still brushing my teeth when he leaves home. I don't understand what earth-shaking activities keep him away from home for so long, holiday or no holiday.

My son works too. He leaves in the morning and hurries back home in the evening. Home is where you find him on weekends. Perhaps the job of the boy with the tousled hair requires him to roam the streets. My neighbour Rama Rao tells me that his name is Anant. He says he doesn't know anything more than that. True, how can people get to know a person who doesn't mix with his neighbours? At least twenty-five households in the neighbourhood recognize my son when they see him, know that his name is Naveen, and that he goes to work every day. He is not a dolt like this Anant. He is a great socializer and I have done all I can to raise him that way. I educated him so that he is competent enough to hold down a job. My son is not a loafer like the boy across the street. He is a homebody. It is another matter that he has no time to talk to me; he is a TV junkie.

Time has not been kind to me. In fact, my condition is quite pitiable. It is not enough that I am given four meals a day—food is not the end-all and be-all for man. Man needs a bit of love, some freedom. Old age has taken away the absolute freedom that had been mine for so long.

'This toothache is unbearable,' I tell Naveen and catch the looks of annoyance on his wife's face. He looks at his wife for guidance, then says to me, 'Is a toothache such a big problem? Eat a betel leaf and gargle or soak a tobacco leaf under your tongue. The pain will disappear. Going to the hospital for every small complaint is a waste of money,' he says and leaves the room.

His behaviour hurts me more than the toothache. My eyes fill. I've already tried every home remedy I could think of. I've done everything short of knocking on the doctor's door. But I haven't told my son about my efforts. How silly it is of me to dream of doctors when my children feel that feeding this old man is charity. I am not allowed to use toothpaste like my son, his wife, and their children. I am given finely ground charcoal. One day, when I couldn't bear the pain and tried to use the toothpaste, I was rewarded with fiery looks from my daughter-in-law.

My son earns enough to lead a comfortable life. Yet I can't turn on the fan even if the weather is warm. I can't ask for food when I'm hungry. It comes at the pleasure of my daughter-in-law. She doesn't allow me to touch my grandchildren for fear of infection. I'd always carried money with me. I like to see the glow in the eyes of my grandchildren when I give them a little money. It's a dream now. The kids have stopped asking me for money because I don't have any.

This is not the end of my tale of sorrow. No one talks to me. Not a word. The children go to school. My son spends time either with his wife or the TV. His eyes greedily fall upon the TV in the corner but cannot see the presence of his father in the room. If by any chance I spill water or coffee, my daughter-in-law uses words that can kill. My son and his wife consider it a waste to spend a single penny on me. Of what use am I to them? None. Silence is my best friend. There's nothing more frightening in life than loneliness.

I am sure that Anant from across the street treats his mother no better than my son and family treat me. This is the condition of many old people today. If I happen to meet God, I'll ask him to explain why human relations are in such a sorry state.

One evening, I was plodding home with a big bag of vegetables when I saw Anant pull over by the curb on his Honda bike and talk to a gentleman. The boy was wearing the same striped shirt with sleeves folded up over the same black trousers; dishevelled hair and that look of nonchalance that had made him turn his eyes away from me. The fellow doesn't have a sense of responsibility; a sense of what is right. Why do such people exist? To eat and loaf around? I brooded on this matter until I reached home.

That evening my son and his family went to a movie theatre. In the compound of the house opposite, Anant's wife was picking flowers in the garden. She aroused pity in me. I'd never seen her going out with her husband. She'd stay at home all day, toiling in the kitchen but Anant was always out, no Sunday, no time off during the weekend or holidays. Always on the road. I wondered how she puts up with it. But her face doesn't show traces of any such sorrow. She is always smiling and talking to neighbours who come over to pick flowers from the garden.

It was ten in the night by the time my son, his wife, and children returned from the theatre. On such occasions, I had to wait until their return, however late, to eat dinner.

Next morning, my son said, 'Daddy, I want to tell you something.' I looked at him, puzzled and apprehensive.

'Your daughter-in-law has received a job offer. If both of us go to work, we can make a lot of money,' he said.

Where was the need for her to go to work? I failed to understand this. Nor could I understand why he was telling me about it. My son was very well off. The house we live in would fetch lakhs of rupees as a result of a recent surge in real estate prices. There was also the prosperous farmland that I'd owned and cultivated for decades that would fetch a fortune. In fact, every year it brings in a ton of money from the lessees. I said so to my son.

'Why should we say no to a good job with a good salary?' he asked.

'As you please,' I shrugged.

'You may have to be alone at home when we go to work and the children to school. You'll get bored. So, we thought of a plan,' he said.

I anxiously waited to hear his plan. Was I not lonely already? What's new?

My son took a deep breath and said, 'We want to put you in an old age home. If you are sick, or fall down, there would be somebody to help you.'

I felt my heart stop for a second and then resume beating. I'd never thought that I'd hear such words from my son. I'd always found time to serve my father despite the hard, punishing work on the farm I had done all day. Those days of such affection, such devotion and love are mere memories now.

I used to run to doctors if my son showed the slightest sign of fever. He would dance and play on my chest when he was a baby. I had taught him his first words. I remembered every hardship I'd endured to build a good future for him; I had spared no cost in fulfilling every whim of his. Those memories pierced my heart now.

I didn't say anything. What is left to say when he regards his father as a hindrance and wants to disown his parent? Whatever he said of his reasons, his main goal must be to get rid of me. Whether it was his idea or his wife's, I didn't care—I just had to get out of that house.

'Don't bother taking me to the ashram. I'll do it myself,' I told him.

My heart burnt and erupted like a volcano. I couldn't sleep that night. I packed all my clothes and personal things into a suitcase and walked out of the house. All I had in my pocket was a twenty-rupee note that I'd found accidentally a long time ago. I'd saved it in case I needed it.

Anant, across the street from me, started his Hero Honda and even though he saw me with the suitcase, didn't offer me a lift. He gave me the same disdainful look that he had before. 'At this rate, his mother too will end up in the ashram one day,' I thought vengefully.

I found an autorickshaw and asked the driver if he knew of any old age homes in the city. 'If you have money there are five-star homes for the rich, with all facilities. For the poor and orphaned, there is Viswambhara. Where do you want to go?' he asked. I decided to go to Viswambhara. The auto took me to a place which was on the outskirts of the town. I paid the autowallah and walked into the ashram with my bags. I found the manager's office, told him my story, filled in the forms, and became...an inmate.

The rooms at the ashram are built around a large leafy area full of old, very old trees, and secured by a boundary wall. There are several benches in the large yard for the senior citizens to sit on, relax, and chat. More rooms are under construction. It is like a haven for the elderly.

I walk around the ashram and find another row of rooms, a school for orphaned kids. The children get free food. Both the old and the young seem to be happy and without a care in the world.

There is a lot of camaraderie among the old people and they regard the children as their own grandchildren. Everyone seems engaged and fully invested in the business of living. I'd always thought the loss of interest in living was the most destructive. There was no sign of that anywhere on the ashram campus.

A day after my admission to the ashram, I chanced upon a news item with a heading that said 'Whither Humanity?' Under the heading was a picture of two old men sprawled on the floor of a bus shelter, outside the government hospital. One of them, according to the story, was dead. The other person was on its brink. Nobody had alerted the municipal staff to the plight of the survivor. I hoped that some Good Samaritan would get the dead man cremated with due respect.

Next day's paper answered the question of the previous day with a jubilant, 'When Humanity Blossomed!' The report said that in response to the previous day's news item, Anant, the founder of Viswambhara, had the survivor admitted to a hospital and personally supervised the cremation of the deceased man. The report also praised Anant for the work of his organization. Next to the report was a photo of Anant in action. I was surprised to see this Anant was the boy who lived in the house across from my son's, the same Anant that left home at sunrise and returned late after midnight.

My eyes remained riveted on the picture—the scales fell off and the truth emerged like the sun from behind a dense shroud of clouds.

The next morning, Anant and the man he'd taken to the hospital got out of an auto at the entrance to the ashram. The old man, leaning on Anant's shoulder for support, was met halfway by two ashram helpers who relieved Anant, the boy who was singularly focused on fulfilling his life's goal and nothing else.

I entered my room and pulled out my suitcase from under the bed. I took out the title deed for my farm, and the passbook. I went looking for Anant, and when I found him, handed him the documents and said, 'Here…I'm donating my property worth lakhs of rupees to the ashram. Please let me share in your joy by supporting this ashram you've created.' He accepted my gift humbly and with utmost respect.

That was the golden moment when life revealed itself to me.

SIGNATURE
JAJULA GOWRI

The bell rang at nine in the Lothukunta primary school. At once, all the children assembled in the school quadrangle and formed queues, each representing a class. After the school pledge was read out, they trooped into their classrooms. When the teachers were about to leave the staff room for their classes with the attendance registers in their hands, the headmaster asked teachers of the fourth and fifth grades to stay back.

He handed out a set of forms to the teachers and told them to distribute them to students belonging to the Scheduled Castes and Scheduled Tribes. The children had to fill them up and return them within a week. Lakshmana Rao and Annamma picked up the forms from the headmaster and left for their classrooms.

After he'd finished his lesson, Lakshmana Rao asked children from Scheduled Castes and Scheduled Tribes to raise their hands. The children looked at him blankly.

'What are Scheduled Castes, sir?' a boy asked.

'Are there Malas or Madigas or other such castes in the class?' the teacher asked.

The children were still perplexed.

'You stupid kids, you don't know your caste?' the teacher asked, surprised.

'No,' they said shaking their heads from side to side.

'What is a caste, sir?' a girl asked.

The teacher didn't know what to tell the children.

'Take the forms home and get your parents to fill them. You'll get a scholarship of forty rupees if you're eligible,' the teacher said.

The mention of money made the children happy, though they still didn't understand what a caste was.

After the lunch hour, Lakshmana Rao met the headmaster and told him of the problem. The headmaster saw Annamma coming in, smiled, and asked her, 'What about you?'

'Just two kids took the forms, sir,' she said.

'You're in a better position. Lakshmana Rao drew a blank.'

'It is not that different in my class. They're kids after all. What do they know about caste? I think we're sowing poisonous seeds of caste in their young minds,' said Annamma.

'I agree. But this is an order from high up above. We have to obey,' the headmaster said and passed the admission book to her.

'This book has all the admission details about the kids. Identify the SC and ST students and give them the forms. We'll have to send them back within ten days. Do it quickly,' the headmaster said.

Ramudu was one of the students in fourth grade that picked up the forms. His eyes glowed when he read through it. The thought of forty rupees every month lifted his spirits. He went home, where he excitedly told his mother, 'Ma, if we fill and return these scholarship forms, we will get forty rupees.'

'What is a scholarship form, son?' she asked.

'I don't know. My teacher told me we'll get money,' said Ramudu.

Ramudu showed the piece of paper to her. 'This is the form. Only Scheduled Caste students get it. The teacher asked me about our caste. What is caste, Ma?'

'Caste means some people are high and others are low. That's all,' the mother said.

'What is our caste, then?'

'We are Madigas, son.' She was surprised he didn't know that.

'How should I know? You never told me. Neither did father,' Ramudu said loudly.

'Let's ask your father,' said Mallamma and took the form to

Rajaiah sitting outside.

'Ayya, Ramudu got this form from the school. See what it is,' Mallamma handed the form to her husband.

Rajaiah took the paper and scrutinized it from every angle. He couldn't make out anything. However, he had a vague idea of what it could be.

He said, 'Nothing. Last year Lachumanna's son also got this form. We have to write our name, our caste, and our address and sign it. That is easy enough. But we need the signature of an officer to confirm our Madiga status. How strange! They treat us like Madigas all the time, but want the signature of a high caste man to prove that we are Madigas! How would they know we're Madigas? Is our caste stamped on our face?' Here, he paused. '"What is your caste?" The babus ask. "Where is the evidence?" After all this fuss, the babu doesn't sign the form unless you bribe him. We don't know all their rules because we didn't go to school.'

'Don't ramble. Just tell me who needs to sign the form,' his wife said impatiently.

'I'm coming to that, woman. A doctor or an engineer or any big officer. They must be government employees. To hell with this fuss, just throw it in the dustbin,' Rajaiah said in disgust.

The boy worried that his father was blowing off a chance for forty rupees.

'Enough of your advice,' the wife said angrily and snatched the form from him. Disheartened, the boy pleaded with his mother, 'Please get a Babu's signature somehow, Amma. We'll get the forty rupees.'

His mother thought of all the chores piled up for her and shouted at the child, 'It can wait. Don't harass me!'

Defeated, the boy retired to a corner of the house to sulk. When his mother called him for food, he refused to eat in protest.

His father would have nothing of the boy's tantrums. He said, 'Don't humour him. Let him starve.'

'Why don't you keep quiet?' his wife snapped at him. She brought a plate of food to the boy and pleaded with him to eat. He refused.

'Okay, we'll go to Lachumanna in the evening. First eat some food, my child,' she caressed her son's head, and finally managed to get him to eat.

She cleared the dishes and left for Lachumanna's place in the darkness. She stood at his door and called out, 'O, Lachumanna.'

Lakshmayya came out. He found Mallamma at the door and asked, 'How are you, sister? How come you are visiting us now, so late in the night?'

'Nothing much, brother. The school gave this form to Ramudu. Please tell me how to fill this form,' she pleaded with him.

Lakshmayya saw the form and said, 'Oh, this form! Ravi got it last year. We made several rounds of the government dispensary but nobody signed it. In the end, I gave twenty rupees to some doctor and got him to sign it. But that doctor is not there now.'

'Okay, I'll go to the government dispensary then and try,' she said and went home.

Next day, she skipped work and walked down to the dispensary, with her son in tow. There was a big line of patients to see the doctor. She waited for some time. More people began joining the queue. In despair, she went home.

On the second day, Mallamma again skipped work and trudged to the dispensary. This time, the doctor came at nine and the line began moving. When her turn came she stepped in with a mixture of fear and desperation. Her boy was with her.

'Who is sick and what is the problem?' the doctor asked brusquely.

'Our health is all right, madam,' Mallamma said timidly.

The doctor moved uneasily in her seat and said, 'Why did you come here if everything is all right?'

She pushed her son towards the doctor and said, 'He got this form from the school. It will get him a small scholarship. It needs to be signed. Please sign it, madam,' the mother entreated the doctor and placed the form before her.

The sight of the form irritated the doctor.

She yelled at Mallamma, 'Are we here to sign these forms or examine patients? Why do you waste our time?'

She then called the orderly and shouted at him, 'What are you doing there at the door, letting in such people? Send them out first!'

The orderly rushed in and dragged the mother by the elbow and her son by the collar, abusing them all the way out. 'Get out, you bastards.'

Frightened, Ramudu hugged his mother and began crying. But Mallamma was in no condition to console her child. Overcome by exhaustion, she collapsed under a tree nearby. But her determination to get the form signed had not lessened.

It was twelve in the afternoon when the last patient left the dispensary. Mallamma sat under the tree, disinclined to leave. A compounder approached her and said, 'What is the matter? I've been watching you since morning hovering around here.'

The compounder pretended to take pity on Mallamma who was crying helplessly. He took the form from her and said, 'I'll get the doctor to sign this. It will cost you thirty rupees.'

'We're poor people living on daily wages. How can I find so much money? I didn't work for the last two days waiting here and lost eighty rupees. The boy lost two days at school.'

'How does it matter to me? Get me the thirty rupees if you want a signature. Nobody does it for free,' the compounder said.

The boy's heart sank when he heard the compounder's words. He became anxious and told his mother, 'Why don't you pay the sir what he wants?'

'Please, for the boy's sake show some mercy, sir. I can't manage to raise thirty. Accept twenty, my lord,' she appealed to the compounder.

The compounder looked around to see if anyone was watching. He said, 'Okay, put that money in this paper, fold it, and give it to me without anyone noticing.'

Mallamma took out a twenty-rupee note from the pleats of

her sari. She folded it in a paper and passed it to the compounder.

He took the money and said, 'Now tell me the names of the kid, his father and where you live.'

He scribbled down the information Mallamma gave him on a piece of paper.

'Come here tomorrow, same time. Don't come in the morning. Too many people watching,' the compounder warned her.

Poor Mallamma looked at him piteously and said, 'As you say, sir. But please get this done somehow. God will be kind to you.'

She then plodded home, her son walking behind her.

That night Rajaiah picked a fight with his wife.

'Nee yamma, you've bunked work for two days and that fellow bunked school. I told you such things are above our means. Did you listen? If you don't go to work tomorrow I won't keep quiet,' he said glaring at her.

'What's your problem? I wasn't sitting around, was I? Did I loaf around the town? You are not willing to get this done. And you won't even let me do it? I did it for the boy's welfare. Is that such a bad thing? Like God, the compounder helped us today. It will all be over by tomorrow. We return the paper to the school and the boy will get the scholarship money,' she said. But she didn't tell him that she'd paid a bribe to the compounder.

On the third day also Mallamma didn't go to work. She went to the dispensary at eleven and stood outside the gate in the sun. The compounder emerged from the dispensary after everyone left. The mother and son greeted him.

Peeved at the twosome meeting him so openly, the compounder said sharply, 'You could have been more discreet and stood to a side. I'd have come to you.'

He took out the form from his pocket and handed it to them.

The mother and son accepted it gratefully, pressing the paper to their eyes as if it were God's gift. 'God will bless you, sir,' they said and went home.

On the fourth day, Rajaiah and his wife went to work, and the boy to school. Lakshmana Rao remembered Ramudu hadn't come to school for three days. The teacher gave him two strokes with his cane and asked him to sit in a chair posture with his back against the wall and knees bent. Compared to the misery of the last three days, that punishment made no impression on Ramudu.

Just before the second bell the teacher asked the kids if anyone had brought their signed scholarship forms. Everyone shook their head.

Disappointed, the teacher told them to bring the forms the next day because there were only three days left for the deadline. He picked up the attendance register and walked out.

Soon after the teacher's exit, Ramudu came out of the chair posture and ran to him saying, 'Sir, sir, here is my form, sir.' He gave the form to the teacher. Lakshmana Rao accepted the form, and affectionately pressed Ramudu's shoulder. The boy's eyes shone with joy. He turned and looked back over his shoulder at the teacher, beaming with pride.

For a moment, he imagined he'd grow up to become a teacher and sign the roster. But his eyes were fixed on the lively parrot perched on the mango bough, his ears tuned to its happy chatter.

A MOTHER'S DEBT
MOHAMMED KHADEER BABU

The mud stove blazes with a sudden burst of anger. The fuel crackles, aided by a melancholic wind blowing across the backyard from the neem tree, a mute witness to life and death in that grief-stricken house. Nazeer squats, overwrought, before the fire, unmindful of the heat of the sun. Her mind wanders over what had happened, a pneumatic drill boring through her soul, jarring every bone in her body. An owl hoots repeatedly from the neem tree filling the air with sounds of distress.

'Go sit inside. I'll take care of the hot water,' says Aunt Basheer, bracing to place the heavy cauldron on the stove. Nazeer sits motionless, deaf to Basheer's words, and stares vacantly into the shape-shifting fire as though looking for answers to her son's death.

'Go in, Sister.' Basheer raises her voice, willing it to persuade Nazeer to go inside where the body of her barely twenty-year-old son rests, cold and lifeless, oblivious to the grieving circle around it. Nazeer makes no move. Basheer is concerned at this strange unresponsiveness, afraid that the tragedy has disoriented her sister.

Nazeer has been like that since sunrise, spent and remote, without uttering a word or even a cry. She sits like a woman petrified by a curse. The mourners want her to cry without restraint, hoping that would release her from the agony of bereavement and maternal grief. But she chants a prayer that Allah should be kind enough to gift another birth to her son.

'Are you listening?' Basheer says in a tone of gentle admonition. It drives Nazeer deeper into her shell, like a frightened tortoise retracting its head.

'Why do you deny me the satisfaction of preparing the hot water for my child's last bath?' Nazeer moans in pain when her sister tries to help her to her feet. Nazeer's heart-rending words release the grief bottled inside Basheer.

'He has gone beyond recall. To Allah he belonged and to Allah he has returned.... Do you also want to follow him?' asks Aunt Basheer in an unsteady voice and caves in, wailing and holding her head.

Aunt Nazini hears Basheer's anguished cry. She comes rushing to the backyard and finds Basheer on the ground, crying. She worries that this will aggravate Nazeer's misery. She remonstrates, 'Stop this drama, why do you cry as if you've lost *your* son? The ordained end has come; he's gone. All of us will have to go to Him one day. Go collect some jujube leaves for the last bath.'

Nazini sends Basheer away and turns to Nazeer. She entreats her, 'What are you doing here, my dear? Go sit with your son before he's borne away and fill your eyes with him. He won't be here too long.'

But soon unable to see the wrenching grief of her sibling, she consoles her and says softly, 'Get up, my child, my helpless child,' and takes her inside the house, now teeming with mourners and condoling neighbours.

They place Shafi's body on a string cot with his head turned to face Mecca. Next to his head, joss sticks burn silently in a glass tumbler held down with rice grains. Their fragrance soon fills the modest house.

People trickle into the room in twos and threes. Draped in white robes and wearing grave expressions, they stand in silence, their heads bowed. One man breaks the silence, whispering to the man next to him 'How could Allah take away such a young boy?'

The man replies, 'To Allah belongs what He took, and to Him belongs what He gave. Who are we to question His deeds?'

A boy next door brings in glasses of tea sent by his mother and offers them to the mourners. Nazini, Basheer, their daughters, and their children hover around the cot, staring into the void. Other friends and neighbours join them, holding glasses of untouched tea.

Shafi's sister Shamim stands by the cot to uncover her brother's face whenever a visitor asks for a last look. When she notices that her brother's eyes are not closed, she gently presses the eyelids down. Every time she reveals his face to a visitor, she weeps afresh.

'What a sinner I am to survive, after you have gone!' Shamim sobs.

Shafi was born after Shamim; she had raised him as her own child. She is not able to bear the grief of seeing that child die and become a memory.

'Quiet, my child, if you break down in this manner how will the younger ones cope with the loss? Get up…and take that girl away too,' Shamim says pointing to Salma. She has been crying since morning, and losing consciousness. Her grief increases when she learns that Shafi had taken her name in his last moments. Could she have even imagined that her dear brother, who had overseen her marriage, would die so young?

'It was not in my destiny to hear your last words. What was it that you wanted to tell me?' she says and slides into hysteria. 'Shafi, you're leaving us without experiencing a single joy in your life, a single celebration!'

Friends of Shafi's father fear that the sight of his grieving children would further crush the old man. They whisk him out to a tea stall, make him sit on the bench outside, and talk to him of this and that to divert his mind from the tragedy.

After a while Khader, Aunt Basheer's husband, arrives in a rickshaw. He brings with him the kafan, the shroud. He goes in and hands it to the children, asking them to wash it and get it ready.

'Oye, it's almost three o'clock now. We have to move the body to the mosque before the afternoon prayers and from there to the burial ground. Is the water ready to bathe the body?' he asks his wife.

With his words he unintentionally causes the mourners to raise the pitch of their wailing.

'Oh my child, have the sands of time run out so soon for you?' The elder sister, Shamim, starts bawling and beating her bosom.

Nazini takes Khader aside and asks, 'What's the hurry? Can't we keep the body for a little while longer?'

'But why?' he snaps.

'Shouldn't we wait for Zeenath? How can you commit the brother to dust without his sister taking a last look?'

He holds his head helplessly.

'Okay. I'll go check on the arrangements at the burial ground,' he says and leaves.

A neighbour of the family calls Khader aside and tells him, 'Please call me if you need money or any kind of help.'

'Thank you, brother. I know we can rely on you,' Khader replies and moves away.

It is half past three. Relatives from Ramayapatnam and Nellore and friends from Ravooru have arrived for the last look. Everyone has arrived, except Zeenath. They had called Zeenath's husband at Bezwada where he works in a factory, informing them of the death and asking them to come immediately. But it takes at least five hours to reach Kavali from Bezwada. She should be here any time now, they think.

'I have checked, there's no traffic jam at Singarayakonda. She'll be here any moment,' says Riyaz, Aunt Basheer's son, who has just unloaded a basket of garlands made of jasmines and maroon marigolds from a rickshaw. What an irony, he thinks. Shafi, who should have sported a wedding sehra on his head made from these flowers, will now be covered with them on his journey to the burial ground.

Nazini suppresses a surge of last-minute emotions, and says, 'Somebody go check at the bus station for Zeenath.'

The words have barely left her lips when a rickshaw pulls up.

'Lo. She has come,' cries someone.

As they see Zeenath coming in, the women inside send up a

heart-rending wail. Shamim rises to embrace her younger sister. Aunt Basheer holds Zeenath and laments, 'See Zeenath, see for yourself what your brother has done.'

Who knows how bitterly Zeenath must have cried through the journey, but with one look at her brother's body her grief returns, redoubled. She collapses on to the ground and thrashes her head crying, 'What have you done, Shafi?'

She collects herself after a while, wipes her eyes and asks, 'How did this happen?'

'TB, they say. The boy didn't tell anyone,' explains Aunt Nazini.

'He was coughing badly but your mother thought it was just weakness and didn't think much of it,' Aunt Basheer adds.

Zeenath's heart burns furiously as she hears this. She curses her mother, 'May this Nazeer perish; may she become dust. God hasn't given her the good sense to take the boy to an expert or get him proper medicines. Does her duty end once she consults a compounder or buys him some cheap herb? Is that enough to keep death away? Shouldn't death visit such a mother soon?' Zeenath rails.

Aunt Nazini intervenes to calm her down, 'Please don't talk like that, Zeenath. They didn't know that his organs had started rotting until the symptoms showed up. By then it was too late. Nazeer did whatever she could. She'd have given her life if she'd known how fatal the disease was.'

Zeenath looks viciously at Nazeer, who, unable to meet her daughter's eyes, covers her head.

'Don't tell me what my mother is. Did she ever let us buy the medicines we needed? She'd say, "Buy whatever ten rupees can buy. Don't talk of tests and such fancy stuff."'

Nazini intervenes with a frown, 'You think that these tests are a joke? They cost thousands of rupees. Do you think we could afford them?'

'You don't know Nazeer. She didn't show any concern even when his condition became serious. She didn't allow him to look after himself. The minute he came home from work she'd run her hand through his pockets and take whatever money he had.'

'What should he care about, his health or his home?' counters Basheer.

'I knew about it a month ago. I didn't tell Nazeer. I told Shafi that he needed nobody's permission to check into the Madanapalle TB sanatorium. The damned thing will be cured in two months. We'll manage the money somehow, I told him so many times. No, he wouldn't listen! He said that that would be a burden on the family,' says Riyaz.

'Why Madanapalle? Resting at home could have cured it. Did she allow him time to relax? No! She'd drive him to work even when he took a day off to take rest. What can you say of a woman who threw out all his medicines and took him to Kanumuru dargah? After three nights there, he came home and collapsed. He never recovered after that,' says Basheer.

'I knew it! My mother is a heartless woman. She dragged the seriously sick boy from place to place until he could take it no more. Otherwise, he might have lived a few more days.' Zeenath weeps.

Not a word escapes the lips of their mother who sits with her head bowed. These angry words travel outside the room and start a flutter of gossip among visitors who have come to give their condolences to the family.

'Have you heard anyone dying from TB nowadays? It is not incurable,' says a neighbour.

'They should have consulted Dr Rahimtullah and saved the boy,' says another.

The debate ends abruptly when they see Aunt Nazini come out of the house looking for Khader.

Khader comes in with four persons from the mosque. They'll preside over the last act.

'It's time for the last bath,' he shouts at no one in particular.

The women rise from their place and make way for the men to

get to the cot. The men lift Shafi's body, carry it to the backyard, and place it on a wooden pallet. They curtain it off with a patchwork of old clothes, lest women see the body and cry afresh.

As the final moments approach, Shamim and Zeenath begin to cry loudly.

Nazeer moves to Uncle Khader's side.

'What?' he asks, irritated.

'He's not used to bathing in very hot water. Please make sure the water is lukewarm,' she pleads.

His eyes fill, he says, 'It'll be done.'

The bathing ceremony begins and, keeping with tradition, jujube leaves are mixed in the hot water. Khader chants 'bismillah' and is the first to pour water over the boy's body. While Shafi's emaciated frame gets bathed, the onlookers become emotional. They pray that the bath should miraculously bring him back to life.

'Bring his father. He has to pour water on the child's body,' says Khader.

Shafi's father is wandering on the street, crying like a man gone mad. He can't bring himself to do his part. Riyaz coaxes the old man, and passing his arm around his waist, brings him to the backyard. The old man grabs the vessel but drops it at once at the sight of his son's body. He cries, 'Ore Shafi, tell me how are we going to live without you?'

Though the relatives take him away at once, they find it impossible to calm him down.

In his day, the old man had been a big landowner, a beacon of hope for people in distress. Though he migrated to Kavali from Vadakampadu, he continued farming. All his wealth vanished in a single year of tobacco blight. What little was left went to fund the weddings of the daughters, Shamim and Zeenath. By the time Shafi was fifteen, the family was in deep debt. The boy became the chief breadwinner. He kept accounts for a shoe shop. Later, he ran an itinerant shoe business. That is how he contracted TB, on his travels.

He never told his parents. Just as he was considering treatment, he had to find money to get his sister Salma married.

Shafi is now given the jujube leaf bath. The body is brought inside the house from the backyard and is laid on a palm reed mat. The womenfolk start an ululation as Shafi is being dressed in the robes of a bridegroom before being placed in the coffin. They apply kohl to his eyes, rub camphor on his sides and spray perfume and rose water on the body.

'My child, why are you headed to the burial ground wearing the finery of a bridegroom?' cries Aunt Nazini. The rest join the dirge.

Unable to bear the cacophony, Khader shouts at them to stop.

'What's the point in crying now? Will he come back?' he asks them and gently calls Nazeer to the boy's body. When she doesn't move, he goes to her and helps her to where the body is.

'Please start,' the man from the mosque suggests to Nazeer.

She looks at him dazed, in a state of incomprehension.

'Why do you stare like that? You have to give the gift of milk to your child,' says the man.

As the meaning dawns on her, she weeps uncontrollably.

'No, I can't. I can't.' She shakes her head. The grief locks her exhausted body in a violent fit.

The women are stunned that a mother should evade her duty towards her son like this. They stop crying and gaze at her in dismay.

'Enough of your crying. Why don't you utter the few words, without fuss, to free your son from the debt he owes you?' bawls out Aunt Nazini.

One of the mourners explains to a Hindu friend of the family, 'See, the last journey can't start without the mother's absolution. It was her milk that the boy was fed on as an infant. He is indebted to his mother for this. Only she can release him from that debt. This is the significance of the last ritual when a Muslim predeceases his mother. The child now belongs to Allah and the mother has to utter these words: "My child, you grew up on my milk. You are therefore indebted to me. You are leaving this world before me with the debt unredeemed. Before all those present, I declare that I'm releasing you from that debt and as a token I'm gifting you this milk." For the dead child to attain salvation it is mandatory for the mother to give him this release.'

'The cortège has to leave, do it,' shouts Nazini, again.

'There's no deliverance for your son if you don't do it, stupid woman,' chides Basheer.

'Mother, this is no time for drama,' says Shamim.

In response to these pleas, the mother merely shakes her head. Everyone takes turns persuading her to utter the words that will absolve her son but no one dares to scold her.

She silently runs her hands over the boy's body.

'Are you listening?' asks the aunt. When there is no response, she calls Riyaz and tells him, 'My boy, go bring her husband. None but he can make her see reason.'

Word leaks out about Nazeer's strange behaviour. Her husband comes in and at once she hugs him and says, 'Look, I've lost everything. I've killed my son with my own hands.' She cries. Her husband joins her and sobs.

'Quiet, my girl, would we have allowed this to happen had we known it in time? What good is repenting? Go, chant those words,' he tells her gently.

She holds on to his shirt for support and crying louder than ever says, 'No, I can't, my dear.'

'Why?' he asks her in the same gentle tone.

'I knew about his TB from the beginning. He pleaded with me. He wanted to go to Madanapalle. I stopped him. I told him we couldn't manage to feed the family without his income every month. I'm a sinner. But did any one of my accusers come forward to help me marry off my daughters? Is there anyone here who would have fed us for a single day? We placed our lives in the hands of Allah and visited dargahs as if they were hospitals. For sixteen years,

I lived on his sweat and blood and took his life in the end. It is I who am indebted to him,' she cries pathetically.

Who will assuage her grief? Will Shafi's last journey ever start?

FESTIVAL OF LOVE
VEMPALLI GANGADHAR

It begins to drizzle but I am only halfway to where the farmhands' huts are. Why on earth is it drizzling in the afternoon? I look around for cover. I find nothing but a hillock; I scale it. From this height, the land below looks as if covered by a fine turmeric dust. I see jasmines blossom in plenitude. The earth is but a basket of flowers. Raindrops settling on the flowers hum folk melodies, responding to a blustering wind blowing in from the hills. Flowers that carpet the ground float away like tiny boats towards the hill stream. Soon, the intensity of the drizzle abates.

As I climb down, I see her in the distance—Syamala, the village beauty who makes my heart throb. With a basket of jasmines on her head, she is walking on the pathway bordering the hillock. I cannot take my eyes off her. I have to act before my father gets to know that I stalk her path. He'd throw me out if he found out.

A few days earlier, I had asked Peeramma to ask my love to come to the well near the tamarind grove. 'I am not a woman of low virtue to oblige him,' my love had replied. But how will my hot blood quieten? How can I sit still until she becomes mine? Until then her beauty will continue to torment me.

She, in her rain-soaked sari, looks like a slender bough of flowers. I become restless. Had she not been surrounded by other women who come daily to work on the farm, I would've shown her the man I am. Lucky for her, she eludes me this time. She walks away pretending not to have seen me. I stare after her until she disappears out of sight.

It starts drizzling again. I turn around to walk back home. I lie down but I am not able to sleep. I am wrapped in her thoughts. Sambasivudu, my frequent confidant, comes by and sits next to me. We talk of inanities, the weather, local gossip. At last I tell him of my longing for Syamala. He laughs explosively.

'Don't laugh, spit out whatever you have to say. What's there to laugh about?'

Without paying the slightest heed, he keeps laughing. I like Sambasivudu or Sambudu, as he is affectionately known. Though he is older than me by several years, we are close. My father and his friends had found him as a child, abandoned at a carnival. He had nobody to take care of him. He started doing odd jobs for the villagers and working on my father's farm, and was adopted by him over time. A few years ago, he had pleaded with my father to let him work on the jasmine farm. Now, he runs the whole farm. He is one of my favourite people in this world. Everyone calls him 'Thikka Sankarayya', meaning an eccentric person. He doesn't mind. That is Sambudu for you, always happy.

He is still laughing. I use an expletive to cut him short.

'That's okay, you fool. I know why you keep talking about her,' he says, raising his eyebrows suggestively.

'Yes, she will be mine. What of it?'

'Yours? Already? You have figured out everything, have you?' he laughs.

'No, not really. You set it up for me,' I plead.

'Master, please don't drag me into this mess. I have my fields and my work to keep me occupied.'

He gets up, flings his hand towel over his shoulder and walks away.

The girl is all that's on my mind now. What must be on *her* mind?

It is dawn. Someone in the distance is singing the praise of Lord Krishna. It is a song about gobbillu, the balls of cow dung used as kindling during the harvest festival of Sankranti. The voice sounds very familiar. From the terrace, I see young girls making small idols of the village goddess, their protectress, from cow dung, and decorating them with turmeric, vermilion, and marigold flowers.

Even as a child I liked the Sankranti festival. The girls in the village would sculpt a big statue from cow dung, carve out a face by pressing two black seeds into the dung idol's face for eyes, and tuck pink and white oleanders all around. The girls, dressed in bright saris with flower garlands in their hair, would carry that idol on a platter and make rounds of the village collecting money and food. I would accompany them to share the sweet treats given to them by the village folk. 'Are you a girl?' the neighbours would tease me. My mother would always chide me for this.

My attention is brought back to the present when another voice begins singing a different stanza from the song. That's her! It is her voice! She is among the bevy of girls singing and clapping and dancing around the main idol. I want to go down and watch her, but my father is among those witnessing this gaiety. He wouldn't approve.

My mother brings out a sieve full of husked rice and empties it into the bag the girls are passing around. My father asks a farmhand to bring a basket of jasmines. Each girl picks up a handful and tucks the blossoms into the lustrous chignon that all of them sport. In Syamala's chignon the flowers glow luminous like the sun. Her beauty matches their radiance.

I cannot take my eyes off her.

Sambudu joins the group of girls with the pretext of making the dung balls and launches into sly songs that describe Lord Krishna's playfulness around the gopikas, the divine cowherd's entourage of besotted women and girls that follow him wherever he goes. My father, amused, tips Sambudu with cash.

In the evening, I visit the hutments to tell the hut-dwellers that they are to report for work the next day. I hope the stars are on my side and will help me snare my love. I have with me some powdered tobacco for Peeravva, Syamala's elderly aunt. I wonder if she could convince the girl to agree to a rendezvous.

Even before I can approach Peerravva the mongrels in the colony launch an attack on me. I run into a lane, jump over a fence, and land in a water tank. From the other side of the fence the dogs continue to bark. The commotion brings Peeravva and my love to the scene. Syamala begins to laugh uncontrollably. I feel miserable at being seen in this state by her. She stretches her hand to help me out of the muddy pool. I ignore it. She goes back to her hut. I wait.

She comes out of her hut a little later and heads to the Gangamma temple just as the bells start ringing to announce the ceremony of lamps.

'Why is she going now?' I ask Peeravva.

'It is to get the blessings of Goddess Gangamma, master,' she says.

I hear the girl's voice raised in prayer, asking the Goddess for protection.

'It's not going to happen tonight,' I think, 'she has escaped me again.' I return home.

Unable to sleep, I go to Sambudu's hut, where I find him lying on the veranda. He sits up when he sees me. I lie down on the veranda in his spot, and say, 'I can't sleep, tell me a story.' It is a common enough occurrence that he launches into a narration without any further questions.

'Once upon a time, there was a king. His subjects complained that a female spirit, a banshee, was haunting a thicket of tamarind trees in the forest and disturbing the peace with her howling and shrieking. The king rode into the forest one night, and just as his subjects had reported, found the creature sitting and sobbing at the foot of a tamarind tree. At his approach the ferocious creature with glowing eyes and flowing hair raised her head to look at him. Afraid to look her in the eye, he bowed his head and asked her, "O spirit, what is your problem? Why are you haunting my kingdom?" She sobbed and replied, "O king, we women are at the mercy of men and their lust, they have cheated us since times immemorial." The king thought, she is just a woman after all! "I will marry you," he declared. "You men are all the same, even the loftiest of kings, instead of helping us when we turn to you for comfort, you lust after us. Nobody should be born a woman!" With an ear-piercing wail, the spirit vanished.' Sambudu finishes with a flourish.

'Are you trying to tell me something here?' I ask.

'Must be your guilty conscience which makes you think that,' Sambudu laughs.

It is morning when my father sends a servant asking me to come home. When I get there, I find that one of the town's principal landowners is already deep in conversation with my father who asks me to immediately bring from the safe all documents relating to lands on lease, lands sold, and the dry lands near the public hostel.

'Why don't you sell off that jasmine field near that stone hill?' the landowner suddenly interrupts the conversation, looking down at the documents.

'You can buy it if you want,' my father says to him but looks at me. I turn my face away.

'What's the matter? Why don't you answer?' the landowner asks me.

Just then Obulesu, one of our farmhands, comes running.

'What happened?' I ask him with foreboding.

'Our Sambudu has been bitten by a cobra near the fields,' he says breathlessly.

'Is he alright?' I ask.

'What can I tell you, master? He fought hard to hang on to his life but then he began to foam at the mouth, that was it…he died, master.'

All of us run towards the fields. Sambudu is lying lifeless on the jasmine petals strewn by the festive girls earlier.

I am unable to contain myself and cry. My mother faints.

Sambudu's body starts to turn dark and blue. Flies buzz around his mouth.

I look around and find Peeravva, Syamala, and others from the hutments standing around, crying.

'Make sure the last rites are performed quickly, properly,' my father instructs. 'Dig a grave right here, in his jasmine field. Bury him. Build a tomb. Make it grand....' My father is unable to continue. The farmhands begin work on the grave. I can't stand there any longer and leave.

I am not able to sleep at night haunted by Sambudu's memories. I murmur and cry in my sleep.

I have stopped visiting Sambudu's jasmine fields. Obulesu oversees the jasmine fields now. The landowner is still interested in that stretch and meets with my father frequently.

I tell my mother to let my father know that I do not have any objection if he wants to sell the jasmine field. She is silent. But after a while she says with tears in her eyes, 'I like that field very much, my son. Please don't sell it as long as I live.' I understand why.

The very next day, I meet the landowner and tell him firmly that I don't intend to sell the jasmine field.

That afternoon, Peeravva tells me that it is the Molakala Punnami festival that day. I give her half a bag of rice and groundnuts to celebrate with. She hesitates on her way out, and then turns around to invite me to the festival.

'What will I do there?' I ask her.

'Why not, master? You are an eligible young man, ready to wed. The festival is meant for young people. Syamala will be there. There is a grand celebration at the Gangamma temple. Don't forget to come tonight.'

The mention of Syamala makes my blood surge. There is every possibility I could take her tonight.

As I set out for the celebration at the temple, the full moon of the Punnami lights up the night. I hear the booming voice of drummer Guruvulayya summoning the young people.

> You, young ladies,
> have competed and succeeded
> in germinating nava dhanyams (grains),
> nursing them in the warm soil with care.
> You have brought the tender sprouts
> to the temple tonight.
> I pray to Mother Gangamma
> to give each of you a good husband.
> Collect your prasadam,
> the offering of soaked rice,
> sesame seeds, and jaggery
> blessed by the Mother Goddess.
> Give it to your love.
> Take these earthen lamps.
> With thoughts of your beloved
> filling your heart and mind,
> release them on the lake.
> Your wish will be fulfilled!

He concludes his blessing. The drumming and chanting resume.

I figure Syamala too is headed for the lake. 'I will ambush her on the way and pull her into the bushes. Surely, she won't be able to stop me,' I think.

I stick to the bylanes and move surreptitiously under a night sky illuminated by the radiant full moon. 'Tonight I will feed on her beauty,' I fantasize in a frenzy. I take up position behind the bushes and wait for her to pass by me on her way from the temple to the lake. I see a large group of girls coming toward me, holding the earthen lamps. She is among them, her face resplendent in the glow of the lamps. But, at the edge of the lake, she suddenly veers away from the path. The other girls kneel at the lakeshore to float the lamps out into the water.

She is alone now.

I come out of the bushes and follow her unseen. She walks on, oblivious to thorns, stones, and pebbles. She begins to climb the stone hill and heads for the jasmine fields. I am worried—snakes, thorns, and God knows what else lurk in the dark. But I become feckless as my desire for her intensifies. I too climb the hill. A thorn pierces my foot. I remove it and push on even as the blood gushes out. She now climbs down the hill on the other side. I limp on behind her, undetected.

The fragrance of the blooming jasmines in the field surrounds me.

She suddenly stops.

She is crying piteously.

She places the lamp on the ground.

She is standing by Sambudu's grave.

She breaks her glass bangles on the grave and rubs the vermilion off her forehead.

She cries heart-wrenchingly.

She places the offering on Sambudu's grave, along with the lamp.

I collapse on to the ground.

Suddenly, it begins to drizzle again.

THE CURTAIN
VEMPALLE SHAREEF

Come take a look at our house with three rooms. The front room has no door. My father had plans to fix one but gave them up; only he knows why. The second room has a curtain. It was not there before. It appeared after my sister came of age. More changes soon followed. The third room is the kitchen.

The second room and the kitchen are Sister's legitimate domain. That is where she may eat, sleep, and spend time. No questions asked. Doorless, the front room is out of bounds for her. At night, she is free to float around the room. Father receives visitors and strangers in the front room. When they are there, the curtain of the second room is drawn to foil any peeping toms. Naturally, Father makes sure that the curtain is drawn to its full width. No crack or aperture. Everyone in the family, including Mother and I, obey Father's will.

My grandma is an exception. Despite her age, she doesn't stay at home. Her feet, strong from domestic work, are itinerant. Mother frowns upon Grandma's outings. Old people must sit in a corner and chant the names of Allah and bismillah, they shouldn't move from their place even if there is a deluge—that is Mother's philosophy. Grandma is a heretic. She goes out whenever her feet itch. The slightest acquaintance is enough for her to sit with people and chat for hours. She doesn't recognize our rules.

'Is this a place where humans live or is this a jungle? Where are all the people who live here?' she asks. She is old but always ready to take on anyone, big or small. Defeat or victory doesn't matter. She has an impressive collection of swear words that puts not only women but also men to shame. In our village, no one has ever dared to cross her. They know the consequences.

Despite such a rowdy past, Grandma is scared of Mother, in a way. Not because she would scold her or thrash her, but because she is afraid Mother may not give her food on time. When Grandma was healthy, she could tackle Mother. If there was any problem she would confront Mother, blow for blow, cuss for cuss, and take a bus and go away to the village. She would do odd jobs there for a living, never looking to us for help. Father didn't show much interest in Grandma, not wanting to get mixed up in the Mother–Grandma brawls. Once a fortnight, he would give Grandma some money. Despite that, she had to work hard.

Why Grandma chose this path of rebellion I have no idea. 'My son is useless. He doesn't look after me. Why should I stay with him and eat food stealthily? Outsiders are better than this twerp. I should just sit on the road and spread a mat. People will throw some food at me. Even his children are like him—thieves. They are their mother's children. They listen to every word of hers and repeat every word of hers. They take her side. Is there anyone in the house on my side? Why should I live in such a place?' Grandma lives by nurturing this grouse in her heart.

Last week, Grandma descended with her bags and bundles, perhaps to stay with us permanently. She agreed to not be a problem; she's never had to compromise before like this. Now, she knows she can't fend for herself anymore. Many of her friends in the village remonstrated: 'Go stay with your son honourably. Here, you'll die destitute.' She had to swallow her pride and seek shelter with her daughter-in-law.

'What is this, a game? I close the curtain, you open it. You forget that there is an eligible girl behind that curtain. What is this important work that takes you outside every minute?' Mother raises her voice one day.

'Blasted curtain, gets me into trouble. I forget in spite of myself,'

Grandma spits out what she'd resolved not to.

Mother loses her cool. 'Yes, you don't remember. But you never forget to eat. It is not even nine in the morning and you're ready for breakfast. Can't you remember to draw the curtain when you can remember your breakfast with such alacrity?'

The words wound Grandma. Why kick up a row again? She'd better remember to close the curtain next time, she tells herself. Peace prevails.

Maybe due to old age, Grandma is always hungry these days. She shuttles restlessly between the front door and the kitchen. She hopes to catch the eye of her daughter-in-law who might deign to offer her something to eat. But no, she heaps curses on the old woman instead. In her village, Grandma was an empress, her own master. She came and went at will. There was none to question or control her.

Her daughter-in-law's treatment sets off a monologue by Grandma: 'It is only here, in this stupid town, that these curtains and stupid rules exist. Secretive people. I've never even had to take the veil and observe gosha. In my days, a girl in her periods would be segregated and after the fifth day asked to mind the cattle. My son's neighbours say his girl is ruddy. What ruddy? She is pallid from being shielded from natural air and the sun. The girl is no good. One pregnancy will bring her to her knees. At that age we used to climb trees. We would pluck tender tamarind leaves. Go to the hills and wield an axe like a man. Make the trees cry. Return before sunset with a bundle of wood. People gaped at us. Today's girls are such a good-for-nothing lot. What curtain! Can't help carry even a pitcher of water. Useless girls, these.'

Father comes home in the sun accompanied by the sound of his flip-flops hitting the ground. He catches Grandma in her soliloquy. He draws the curtain aside gently, as though lifting a cover off a sleeping child's face. Then he closes it and it flaps in Grandma's face who was trying to peer inside.

Grandma's anger now is directed at her son. What a weak child he had been; always trailing behind her holding the end of her sari. Now, look at him today. No concern for all she'd been through for his sake. Those days wives were scared of their husbands. She'd been no exception. She still remembered the husbandly beatings. She would curse the poverty of her parents who'd palmed her off on that drunkard, a widower to boot. Despicably sick, he had died when the child was just a few weeks old. That had been the beginning of her bad days. Grandma's eyes become moist.

A fly bothers her. Stupid thing, she says and slaps her face to crush it. It flies away.

'I've been sitting outside here in the veranda. The fellow pretends he has not seen me. Just barges inside. He doesn't even ask me: "how are you, did you have breakfast?" He will turn to dust,' she curses him. 'A woman and a widow at that, I never cowered in front of anyone while bringing him up. This fellow, look at his manly moustache, and yet he is afraid of his children. Can't even marry his daughter off. Bloody eunuch.'

Grandmother, spoiling for a fight, asks my father, 'Why do you hide your daughter behind the curtain?'

'I don't have the money for a big dowry. Hundreds of thousands of rupees. If we let the girl run wild, who will marry her? It's no joke to get this girl married. Somebody will be willing to marry her if she is docile and learns a few Urdu words, and that's enough. "The dowry is not much but at least the girl has been raised properly," they'll say,' father replies.

Grandma understands now why her son had banished his daughter behind the curtain. He wanted to pass off as a gentleman and escape paying dowry. He has no interest in anything other than observing gosha. He doesn't respect his own mother. All his tradition is confined to enforcing gosha.

The fly returns and tries to land on Grandma's face. It's a bad omen. She stretches out her hand, catches the fly, squashes it and throws it out into the street. The fly falls supine onto the ground.

Grandma rises from her place on the veranda and begins the long walk to the government hospital. She'd complained of chest pain to her son several times. He'd brought her some pills once or twice and let the matter rest there. But she needed to go to the hospital now.

Whenever she goes out, Grandma never covers her chest with a scarf as was the custom of many Muslim women. She merely flings a piece of old cloth like a towel over her shoulder. This had been her habit even in the village.

This time she thinks it better to wrap herself well. She pushes the curtain aside to come inside the house and pick up her scarf. She remembers that it was in the alcove in the veranda and turns back. Her daughter-in-law had thrown all her things out on the veranda as punishment for Grandma's disregard for the curtain rule. Cursing her daughter-in-law, Grandma collects her scarf, tucks it under her arm, climbs down the steps of the veranda, and starts walking on the road. She hasn't bothered to drape the scarf on her shoulder. Perhaps she believes modesty isn't a pressing concern for an old hag. She fixes a broken strap on her worn-out slip-ons with a safety pin. Her chest pain is more intense that day. She walks to the hospital haltingly, carrying her arched frame, moaning and whimpering.

Carpenter Kasim notices her outing. Father and Mother are trying to arrange Sister's marriage to a relative of Kasim. He happens to see Grandma on her way to the hospital. He was on another matchmaking errand. Even though it is none of his business, he stops and asks her where she's going. She starts a conversation.

'Going to the government hospital, my son. My son never took me to the doctors there. Last time I went by myself, they gave me a shot. I'm going to get one again,' she says.

He doesn't ask her why she's going to the hospital. After his errand, he stops by at our place and whispers excitedly to my mother and father.

Father boils with rage. Mother too. After some time, Grandma returns home with the scarf tucked under her arm. Father goes berserk at the sight of Grandma returning home.

She hopes that her son will ask where she has been so that she could tell him about the chest pain. That doesn't happen.

Father shouts the moment Grandma steps inside the house. 'Why do you roam the streets like a beggar woman? Can't you wrap yourself in a scarf like a respectable woman till your granddaughter is married?'

Grandma is stunned. But soon she gathers her courage and spits at him, all the venom she had been bottling up.

'Bastard, why're you after me? Tell me, who is the bride, your daughter or me?' Grandma shakes with anger. 'My body is a wreck. I don't know how I will buy all those medicines the doctors have scribbled for me. And now your behaviour? I am not allowed to open my mouth and share my pain. What kind of life is this? You want me to cover my chest as if I have newly sprouted breasts? People will spit on you if they hear this.' Grandma really spits on his face in a fit.

Father loses his senses. He rises and grabs her, but before he can land his fist on her back, Grandma cries loudly, 'Oh, the man has killed me. I'm dead.' Father lets her go.

'Why do you bawl? Shut your trap, you vile woman,' Father shouts.

Still, there is no stopping Grandma. She continues to howl. She provokes him, 'Come, stab me, you bastard. Let me see if you have the guts.'

Father goes after her. He might've killed her if he had stayed there for another minute, but abruptly, he hitches up his lungi and walks out of the house. He tells me on his way out, 'You brat, keep an eye on her; tell me if she goes out without her scarf.'

This warning unsettles Grandma. She cries again, 'Oh God, look at my lot. I had to beg for food going door to door to feed him when a fire razed our hut. Would my son have survived if I'd hidden behind a curtain?'

She recovers soon.

'No, I won't stay here. I'd rather beg or steal,' she says. She packs her things and shuffles off. I stand and stare through tears at the receding figure of Grandma.

ACKNOWLEDGEMENTS

We would like to extend our particular thanks and gratitude to Sahitya Akademi Award winner Smt P. Sathyavati for her constant advice and help in getting in touch with many of the writers. Grateful acknowledgement is also made to the following copyright holders for permission to reprint copyrighted material in this volume. While every effort has been made to locate and contact copyright holders and obtain permission, this has not always been possible; any inadvertent omissions brought to our notice will be remedied in future editions.

'The Night After' by Kanuparthi Varalakshmamma. Translated with permission of S. V. H. Prasad.

'Adventure' by Kodavatiganti Kutumba Rao, translation first published in *1947 Santoshabad Passenger and Other Stories* (Rupa & Co., 2010).

'The Coral Necklace' by Achanta Sarada Devi, translation first published in *1947 Santoshabad Passenger and Other Stories* (Rupa & Co., 2010).

'Yaatra' by Turaga Janaki Rani, translation first published in *1947 Santoshabad Passenger and Other Stories* (Rupa & Co., 2010). Reprinted with permission of Usha Turaga-Revelli.

'House Number' by Kavana Sarma. Translated with permission of Vijayalakshmi Kandula.

'Breeding Machine' by Sheik Hussain Satyagni. Translated with permission of the author.

'Water' by Bandi Narayanaswami. Translated with permission of the author.

'Predators' by Syed Saleem. Translated with permission of the author.

'The Truant' by Dada Hayat. Translated with permission of the author.

'Adieu, Ba' by Baa Rahamathulla. Translated with permission of the author.

'Morning Star' by Palagiri Viswaprasad, first published in *1947 Santoshabad Passenger and Other Stories* (Rupa & Co., 2010). Reprinted with permission of the author.

'Eye-opener' by Chaduvula Babu. Translated with permission of the author.

'Signature' by Jajula Gowri. Translated with permission of the author.

'A Mother's Debt' by Mohammed Khadeer Babu. Translated with permission of the author.

'Festival of Love' by Vempalli Gangadhar. Translated with permission of the author.

'The Curtain' by Vempalle Shareef. Translated with permission of the author.

NOTES ON THE AUTHORS

CHALAM (1894–1979), as Gudipati Venkata Chalam was popularly known, typically wrote on themes related to the unconsummated passions of women, the social consequences of the repression of women's desires, and their real and fantasy lives. His novels include *Maidanam, Sasirekha, Dyvamicchina Bharya, Jeevitadarsam, Brahmanikam,* and *Bujjigadu*. Prominent among his fifteen short story collections are *Jealousy, Aa Raathri, Prema Paryavasanam,* and *Satyam Sivam Sundaram*.

KANUPARTHI VARALAKSHMAMMA (1896–1978) wrote works that figure in scores of short story anthologies in several languages. Yet short story is only one of the literary forms that emerged from her pen. Despite writing many stories, there is only one published collection of her short stories, *Kanyashramam*. Her 'Sarada Lekhalu' is a perfect example of a story told through an epistolary exchange. *Vasumati* is her sole novel. She was also a playwright for All India Radio, a freedom fighter, and a much sought-after speaker. She was the first woman to receive the Grihalakshmi Swarnakankanam and won the Andhra Pradesh Sahitya Akademi Award for best writer in 1967.

KODAVATIGANTI KUTUMBA RAO (1909–1980), or KoKu, was a master of the Telugu short story. His monumental corpus of work includes fourteen story collections, twenty novels, 100 radio plays, and a miscellany of other literary works. He was a scientist by qualification but he edited film journals and the popular *Chandamama* children's magazine.

ILLINDALA SARASWATI DEVI (1918–1998) was born in Narsapur. She published over forty works, including twelve novels, several plays and essays, biographies, and short stories. She also wrote children's literature, including a concise biography of Mahatma Gandhi and *Mahatmudu Mahila* (*Gandhiji's View About Woman*), published in 1969 by Andhra Pradesh Sahitya Akademi. Her other significant works include the novels *Muthyalu Manasu*, *Darijerina Pranulu*, *Tejomurtulu*, and *Akkaraku Vacchina Chuttamu*, and the short story collection, *Raja Hamsalu*. A legislator by profession, Saraswati Devi was one of the founders of Andhra Yuvati Mandali. She won the National Sahitya Akademi Award in 1982 for her short story collection *Swarna Kamalalu*.

ACHANTA SARADA DEVI (1922–1999) has five short story collections to her credit including *Paaripoyina Chilaka* and *Pagadaalu*. She was the recipient of the Andhra Pradesh Sahitya Akademi Award, and was the head of the department of Telugu at Padmavati College for Women, Tirupati.

MADHURANTAKAM RAJARAM (1930–1999) was born in the Damalcheruvu village of Chittoor district in Andhra Pradesh and considered one of the foremost experts in the art of short story writing. In the span of over five decades, he wrote many short stories depicting the lives of middle-class or lower-middle-class people from the Rayalaseema region of Andhra Pradesh. His collection of short stories include *Madhurantakam Rajaram Kathalu* and *Halikulu Kushalama*; he received the Sahitya Akademi Award for the former.

TURAGA JANAKI RANI (1936–2014) was a playwright, short story writer, poet, biographer, and broadcaster with a writing career that spanned more than a half century. Her works include the short story collections *Janaki Rani Kathalu*, *Erra Gulabilu*, and *Navvani Puvvu*, and the novels *Veyyabovani Talupu*, *Sangharshana*, and *Eee Desam*

Oka Himalayam. She was honoured with many awards including Grihalakshmi Swarnakankanam and Telugu University Sahitya award.

KAVANA SARMA (1939–2018) is known to Telugu readers both as a storyteller and as a man of science. A former professor at the Indian Institute of Science, Bangalore, he taught and lectured at universities in the US, the UK, Iraq, Australia, and the West Indies. *Vyangya Kavanalu*, *Kavana Sarma Kathalu*, *America Majili Kathalu*, and *Sangha Puranam* are prominent among his short story collections. He won the Jyeshta award and Telugu University award.

BOYA JANGAIAH (1942–2016) was a playwright, poet, biographer, and short story writer. Jangaiah reaped an enviable harvest of awards and honours: an honorary doctorate from Telugu University, Swarajyalakshmi award, Chaso award, Malayasri award, Visala Sahiti award, Telugu Bhasha award, and the Telugu University award, among others. His short story 'Eccharika' won the Rachakonda Viswanatha Sastri gold medal from Nagarjuna University. *Ippa Poolu* and *Adavi Poolu* are two of his twelve short story collections. Other works include a novel *Jagadam*, and a collection of poems, *Boja Kavitalu*.

SHAIK HUSSAIN SATYAGNI (1943–) is a writer, besides being a legislator, actor, party official, literary activist, and filmmaker. He is the former chairman of the A. P. Forest Development Corporation.

BANDI NARAYANASWAMI (1952–) was born in Anantpur district. He received the 2019 Sahitya Akademi Award for his novel *Saptabhoomi*. His other works include novels, such as *Rendu Kalala Desam*, *Meerajyam Meerelandi*, and *Nisargam*, and short story collections *Veeragallu* and *Gaddalu Adutunnai*. His other awards include the NATA (North American Telugu Association) in 2017, Appajosyula award, N. T. Rama Rao Award, and Kolakaluri Swaruprani Award.

SYED SALEEM (1956–) won the National Sahitya Akademi Award for his novel *Kaaluthunna Poolathota* in 2010. Many of his short stories have appeared in the four collections, *Swati Chinukulu*, *Nissabda Sangeetham*, *Roopayi Chettu*, and *Chadarapu Enugu*. Several of them have been translated into Hindi, Kannada, Marathi, Odia, and English. He also won the National Human Rights Commission award for the English translation of *Kaaluthunna Poolathota*. Saleem has written four novels, and is also a poet with two collections to his credit. His other awards include the Bhasha Puraskar from the Andhra Pradesh government, Madabhushi Rangacharyulu award, and Sahitya award from Telugu University.

DADA HAYAT (1960–) was born in Venkatagiri in Nellore district. His story 'Ahimsa' (translated as 'The Truant' in this anthology) launched his literary career and was translated into many languages. His story 'Maseedu Pavuram' was translated into Hindi by the Sahitya Akademi. He is also an able translator and has translated Telugu works of other writers into English.

ADDEPALLI PRABHU (1963–) was born in Kakinada as Addepalli Prabhakara Rao. He has authored three poetry collections, *Aavaahana*, *Paaripolem*, and *Pittaleni Lokam*. He has written more than seventeen novels, three short story collections, and several poetry collections including several Telugu–English bilingual ones. He is the recipient of the Vummidisetty Sahiti Award.

BAA RAHAMATHULLA (1963–) was born in Santhanoothalapadu in Andhra Pradesh. He is the author of several short story collections including *Baa* and *Maa*; *Baa* has been translated into Urdu. A collection of his poems was published in 2007. He is also a translator and has rendered several English stories into Telugu.

Notes on the Authors

PALAGIRI VISWAPRASAD (1963–) is a journalist by profession, reporting for *Andhra Bhoomi* from Kadapa. His publications include a collection of short stories called *Chukka Podichindi*.

D. K. CHADUVULA BABU (1967–) was born in Jillella in Andhra Pradesh. Babu or Khasim Saheb, as he is also known, began his literary career with writing for children's magazines, like *Chandamama, Bommarillu,* and *Balamitra,* and also for Telugu dailies. He has published several collections of children's stories. One of his stories is included in the high school syllabus in Maharashtra. He won the Uttama Sahitya Puraskaram in 2007 and Sri Venkateswara University's Sahitya Puraskaram.

JAJULA GOWRI (1969–) was born in Hyderabad. Married at a young age, she pursued higher studies in journalism and soon found recognition as a poet and activist. Her works include several short stories and a novel, *Voinam*. She currently holds political office. She has received many awards including the Chaso, Visala Sahiti, Telugu University Sahitya Award, and the Dalit Sahitya Akademi Award.

MOHAMMED KHADEER BABU (1972–) is a journalist and wrote his first story 'Pushpaguchcham' in 1995. He has twice won the Katha Award for 'Zameen' and 'New Bombay Tailors'. His other awards include the Bhasha Samman award and the Chaso Award. Many of his stories have appeared in several anthologies. His published works are *Darga Mitta Kathalu, Polerama Banda Kathalu, Phuppujaan Kathalu, Beyond Coffee,* and *Metro Kathalu*.

VEMPALLI GANGADHAR won the Sahitya Akademi's Yuva Puraskar in 2012. His short story collection *Molakala Punnammi* was highly commended. In 2014, he was the first ever writer-in-residence at the Rashtrapati Bhavan. His novels include *Uranium Palle* and *Nela Digina Vaana*. His numerous awards include the Andhra

Pradesh Cultural Council award, Telugu story National Award, ATA (American Telugu Association) Story Award, Gurajada Appa Rao Sahithi Puraskaram, Vishala Sahiti B. S. Ramulu Katha Puraskaram, and World Telugu Conference's Sahiti Puraskar.

VEMPALLE SHAREEF (1980–) won the Sahitya Akademi's Yuva Puraskar in 2011. Born in Vempalle in Kadapa district, his story collections include *Katha Minar* and *Topi Jabbar*, and a collection of children's stories, *Thiyyani Chaduvu*. A TV journalist, he began his literary career with children's stories. His stories have appeared in many anthologies; some have been translated into English and Maithili. His story 'Jumma' received a special mention in the nationwide competition held by Muse India for regional stories. His awards include the Chaso Award, Karnataka Sahitya Parishad Award, and the Andhra Pradesh Ugadi Puraskaram.